MAYBE ALWAYS

MAYBE, DEFINITELY BOOK 3

ELLA MILES

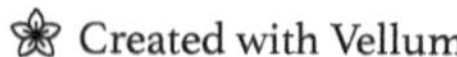 Created with Vellum

FREE BOOKS

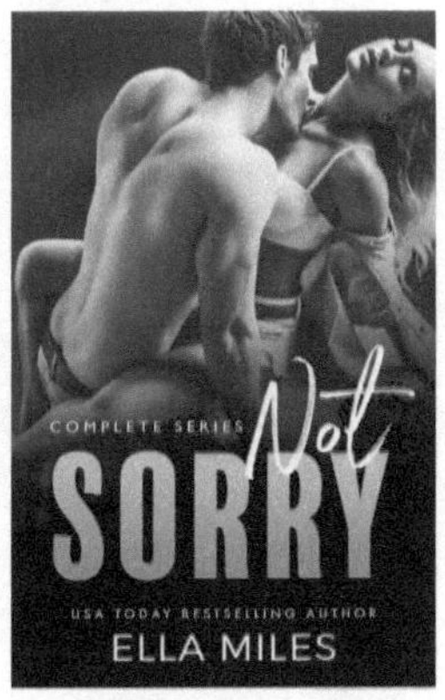

Read **Not Sorry** for FREE! And sign up to get my latest releases, updates, and more goodies here→EllaMiles.com/freebooks

Follow me on BookBub to get notified of my new releases and recommendations here→Follow on BookBub Here

Join Ella's Bellas FB group for giveaways and FUN→Join Ella's Bellas Here

Will one truth set her free?

Kinsley thought she had found the truth, but she is only beginning to discover the real truth about her family. About herself. Her heart and body still yearn for Killian, but she has to keep him safe. The only way to do that is to lie, just like everyone has lied to her.

Killian thought he had everything he ever wanted. He had the perfect girl. He had the perfect job. All that was missing was a ring on her finger. But now both are gone. And the only way to get either of them back is to choose between the girl he loves and the job he feels destined to do. But as he sits in a jail cell he doesn't know how he will get either of them back.

Will Kinsley be strong enough to save herself and those she loves? If so, at what cost?

KINSLEY

"Ma'am, can I get you anything to drink?" the flight attendant asks.

I open my eyes and then immediately yawn. I've been flying for over twenty-four hours with minimal sleep.

"Coffee," I say. I have only about an hour left on this last flight. I need to start waking up.

"Here you go," she says, handing me the coffee.

I take it and set the cup on the tray table in front of me. Next to the coffee are my new passport and the letter my father wrote to me.

I flip the passport open again and read the name, Hannah Grove. I got the passport from the same abandoned building Killian got our previous fake ones from in Tokyo. It was risky. I didn't know if Killian or the FBI would check there. Even if they do, I paid the man almost ten times the amount the FBI usually does to ensure loyalty to me and not them. They can't know where I am or where I'm going. Although I know they will figure it out soon.

I told Killian I was going to turn myself in. When I got to

the airport, I called the FBI and told them the same. I even bought a direct flight from Dublin to New York.

I just didn't get on it.

I learned from Killian the best way not to be found was to get good and lost. Change passports. Change planes. So that's what I did.

I'm not going to turn myself in. I'm going to Mexico. I'm going to end this. I'm not going to let Killian get hurt for my family. I'm not going to let him lose his job for me. I love him, and I know he loves me, but he can't keep harboring a fugitive. He can't keep protecting me and keep the job that is so important to him. I just hope the FBI will believe Killian is loyal to them and not me.

I shake my head, thinking back to my conversation with Agent Hayes.

"Hello, this is Agent Hayes."

I nervously hold the pay phone in my hand and take a deep breath. I have to tell him. I have to do this.

"This is Kinsley Felton."

Agent Hayes sucks in a breath on the other end of the phone, but his voice is calm when he speaks, "Where are you?"

"I can't tell you that. All you need to know is that I'm buying a flight back home. My flight gets in at eight tomorrow morning at LaGuardia, and then I have a connection to Las Vegas at nine. I'll cooperate. I'll do whatever you want."

"Is Agent Byrne with you?"

"No. He's been tracking me. I saw him in London, but he didn't find me. He's the reason I'm turning myself in. I can't keep living my life, running from the law."

"That's good, Kinsley. Just get on that flight. We will meet

you in New York and fly back with you to Las Vegas. Then we can talk. You aren't in any trouble. We just want to talk."

I know he's lying. He doesn't just want to talk. He wants to arrest me and my grandfather. If only he knew how much bigger this is than just money laundering and tax evasion. It's much bigger. And I'm the only one who can put a stop to it.

"I'll be on the flight," I say.

I sip on my coffee. I don't know if Killian has a chance at staying in the FBI's good graces, but at least he will be safe in the US and not here, trying to protect me. No one can protect me. As much as my father thought he could, no one can. My family is too involved. And as much as I want to just abandon my family, I need to make things right. After I figure it out, I can save Killian's career by making him seem like the hero.

I unfold the letter my father wrote and begin reading it for the hundredth time.

My dearest princess,

If you are reading this, I am no longer with you, and I'm so sorry about that. There is nothing more I wanted than to spend forever with you, protecting you from what I now must tell you. I need you to know, even after you've read the last word on this page, I love you princess. I love you more than everything else in my life even if I wasn't always able to show you.

I don't know how to tell you this, but I have to. I'm not a good person. Your grandfather is worse. Your great-grandfather might have been worse than him. We aren't casino and hotel owners. Not at our hearts. We are criminals. We like greed and money above everything and will do anything to keep it.

By now, you might have found out we are money launderers. We don't pay our fair share of taxes. We have lied and cheated our investors out of money. And, while that is all true, it was just a cover for what we really do.

I can't believe I'm even going to tell you the worst of it because you will never forgive me after I do. You will hate me, and your hatred for me will be valid. I won't be there to defend myself, but you deserve to know who your family is. You deserve to know the truth.

So, here it is. We are smugglers. It started off small. Drugs and guns in small amounts, but it quickly grew. We realized we could make more money doing that than we ever could running hotels and casinos. Then, we found reinvesting the money into our casinos and hotels would make us even more money and keep our real activities hidden.

But the smuggling of drugs and guns soon grew so large, we got even greedier. We wanted more. Always more and more. We never had enough.

So we grew to smuggling jewels, diamonds, anything of value. And that satisfied us for a while until we found out what our partners really wanted, what they would pay top dollar for.

People.

They wanted us to smuggle people.

Our immediate response should have been no, but we couldn't say no because we were in too deep. And, to be honest, we didn't want to tell them no. We wanted the money and excitement that came with smuggling. So, it made no difference to us if we were smuggling drugs, guns, diamonds, or people. They were all the same to us.

I realize now it was a mistake. But, at the time, it was just our next adventure, an adventure we passed down from generation to generation. From son to son.

I didn't realize how wrong it was until I had you, and my

world changed. At first, I thought I could pass the company to you along with all of our illegal activities, but we quickly realized that wouldn't be a possibility. You were too delicate to take over. You would have ruined everything we worked so hard to build.

So, instead, we thought we could pass it on to your husband. But we would have to choose your husband very carefully to ensure we could pass the company on to him.

Finding you a husband became our new mission. Tristan was horrible. We knew he was a druggie and couldn't be trusted around drugs, so we set him up. Of course, that turned into a mess when you were caught with the drugs instead of him. But, in the end, it all worked out. He was gone from your life, and you gave us the deciding power to choose your next boyfriend and who your husband would be. It couldn't have worked out better.

We let you date Eli because he was harmless, but we knew he would never work out.

And then I met Killian. Killian was perfect. Strong, decisive, and loyal. He would do anything I asked of him without a second thought. And I asked a lot of him.

He was strong enough to run the company and keep up with the illegal activities, while still protecting you from them.

We thought we had found the perfect solution.

Except we hadn't. I found out he was FBI. I was going to have to kill him, a man I had grown to love as a son. I was going to have to shoot him in cold blood.

Now, you need to know I've killed before, so it wouldn't have been an unusual thing for me to do, but I've never killed someone I thought would one day be my family, someone my daughter would someday marry.

But I had no other choice. The day came when I had to kill him. I had the gun. I had Killian alone, but I couldn't do it. I couldn't kill him, but if I didn't, we were all as good as dead. You were as good as dead. I couldn't have that.

I had to protect you. That became my obsession. I would do anything to protect you.

So, I made the decision to sacrifice myself and your grandfather to keep you safe. I told Killian I would give him everything he needed to put us away in prison if he swore to keep you safe. He promised, and I believe him.

I haven't told him everything yet, but I will. All he knows about is the money laundering. He's gained my trust though, so I can now tell him the rest. Now, I can tell him everything, and he can help me nail these guys, but it will be at the cost of me and your grandfather going to jail. We deserve it though. And I would do it all again to keep you out of harm's way.

But, if for some reason I die before I get a chance to tell Killian everything, you have to tell him. You have to give him this letter. You have to let him protect you. Promise me, princess, that you will be safe. Your safety is the only thing that matters to me.

I included the address to our main smuggling facility in Mexico at the bottom of this letter. I've already laid the groundwork to make sure Killian will be accepted as my successor. He will be able to gain access, and call in the FBI to arrest everyone involved.

I'm so sorry, princess. I hope you can forgive me someday, but I don't know if you will be able to. I'm sorry, but you will be safe.

All my love,
   Dad

I wipe away a tear. I cry each time I read the damn letter.

I didn't even know my father. I knew nothing about him

at all. He wasn't a nice, caring father. He was a criminal who ruined who knows how many people's lives.

If he thought I was going to just let Killian come in and fix all my family's problems, he was wrong. There is no way I'm going to let the man I love risk his life to protect me. Not when I know there is a real chance Killian could be killed if he tried to arrest any of these men. I can't let him die while protecting me, even if it is his job as an FBI agent. I won't let him do that. Not on my account. Not when his cover has been blown.

No, I have to find a way to infiltrate them myself. Once I have evidence that we really do smuggle people, then I can call in reinforcements to arrest everyone.

I fold the letter back up and put it in my pocket. I put the tray table up and sit in silence as the plane lands before I go through the long process of exiting the plane and going through customs. Then, I'll be off to form a plan in a nice hotel; the last nice hotel I might ever stay in.

If only I could find a way to contact my grandfather, then I could easily put an end to this, but I don't even know if he will be in Cancún when I land.

I don't have a choice though. Even if he isn't there, I have to go to the address my father provided. And, when I do, I will be the criminal. Despite my good intentions, there will be no distinction with the law. The FBI will arrest me if I make it out of there alive. And being with Killian will no longer be a possibility. But at least he will be alive and free to continue working as an FBI agent while I pay for my family's sins.

KILLIAN

I FEEL the cold metal handcuffs go onto my wrists, and then it becomes real. I'm being arrested. My career is over, my life is over, and all because I fell in love with a woman I was never supposed to love.

Agent Hayes grabs my arm and begins leading me through the airport.

He's talking to me, but I'm not listening to him. I'm too worried about Kinsley to listen to the meaningless words coming out of his mouth. I already know why I'm being arrested. I'm being arrested for helping her when I shouldn't have.

I made a promise to Kinsley's father that I would protect her above everything else. I would have protected her anyway. And, now, I've failed. I failed the second I let her out of my sight.

Hayes leads me outside to an unmarked black SUV, the same type of SUV I've driven criminals in before. I climb in and realize how uncomfortable it is to sit in a car with my arms stuck behind my back. Hayes buckles me in before climbing into the front seat. I'm surprised when he begins driving without a partner in the seat next to him. He's not following protocol.

I sit up straighter. "Where are we going?"

Hayes glances up to the rearview mirror to look at me. His eyes look sad. "FBI office."

My shoulders slump. "Hayes, you have to listen to me. Kinsley is in trouble. We have to—"

"I know she's in trouble. She said she was going to turn herself in, and then she didn't. Now, she is officially a fugitive. She's facing a lot of jail time."

"That's not what I'm talking about. She isn't safe. You have to let me go. She could die."

Hayes shakes his head. "You don't understand, Byrne. You are in a lot of trouble, too. The office thinks you were harboring a criminal. A criminal you were supposed to be prosecuting. Under the Patriot Act, you could go to jail for life without a trial."

I glare at Hayes. "I thought you were my friend. I thought you were going to help me and keep silent about what you knew."

"I tried. Kinsley called me when I was in Bisson's office. With our boss over my shoulder, I didn't have a choice. He heard everything. And then you called. I had no choice. If I didn't arrest you, they would have arrested me."

"Why aren't you following protocol then? You know you will be reprimanded for not having a partner when arresting a fellow FBI agent. What is the point?"

Hayes's eyes drift down to the steering wheel. "I wanted to talk to you alone. I know I'm the only person who might be able to talk some sense into you. This girl isn't worth losing your career over. You barely know her."

"She's worth protecting though."

"Only because you love her."

"No…"

"No, you don't love her?"

"No, that's not the reason she's worth protecting. She's naive yet strong. Loving yet ruthless. A princess and a warrior. She is a perfect contradiction. But, most importantly, she is innocent and in danger. I don't know about you, but I took an oath when I took this job. I promised to protect the innocent and those in danger."

Hayes sharply turns the wheel. We turn the corner before pulling to a stop in an alleyway. For a second, I think maybe he is letting me go, that I've convinced him, but when he turns to face me with anger on his face, I know he's not going to let me go.

"She's not innocent, Byrne. She's a criminal, just like her family. If she were innocent, she would have been on that flight back home. If she were innocent, she wouldn't have lied to me about where she is going."

"She was lying to protect me!"

"Why would she protect you? She's the one who supposedly needs protection, not you."

"Because that's what she does. She protects the people she loves, no matter the cost."

Hayes sighs.

"You have to let me go, so I can go after her. She could die if I don't."

Hayes narrows his eyes at me. "I can't."

I drop my head, knowing he is my last chance to get free. My last chance to save her.

"Why does she need protection?"

I raise my head again. "Because her family is involved with dangerous people, and she is going to try to stop them. She feels responsible for her family's actions and feels she has to be the one to resolve them even though she carries none of the guilt herself."

"What are you talking about? You went undercover with this family for five years. You never found out anything other than the money laundering, did you?"

"No," I lie. "I never found anything else out."

"Then, what makes you so sure now? She could be lying to you. She could just be setting you up so she and her grandfather have time to hide somewhere we will never be able to find them."

I shake my head. He doesn't get it. He will never get it. I have to find another way to save her.

Hayes' eyes study mine for a long time. The longer we sit here, the angrier our boss, Bisson, is going to be when we finally get to the office. He will think Hayes did something. He will think Hayes is helping me. I can't let that happen. Hayes doesn't deserve to be punished because of me.

"Just take me to the FBI office."

Hayes runs his hand through his hair. "I don't know why I'm going to say this, but I believe you. You obviously believe the girl is in trouble, and I believe you. I can't let you go though, but I can go after her myself. Where is she?"

I stare back into the eyes of the only friend I have at the Bureau. My only friend. But I don't trust him. I can't tell if he is using a technique just to get me to confess where she is or if he is genuinely concerned and will go after her without telling the FBI. So, I keep my mouth closed. I can't trust him. I can't trust anyone but myself when it comes to Kinsley's safety.

"I'm disappointed in you, Byrne," Hayes says. Turning back to the wheel, he begins driving again.

We drive the rest of the way to the FBI office in silence. Hayes parks the car in front of the large building and then walks over to my door. He unbuckles my seat belt and helps me out. He holds on to my arms as he pushes me inside the office building I have walked into countless times of my own volition, but now, I am walking in while under arrest.

I watch the stares as we walk to the elevator. Each person who sees me is one more person I never want to see again. Each person's face wears the same expression—disappointment. Everyone is disappointed in what I did. In their eyes, I let the Bureau down, and I'm a criminal.

Everyone has always thought I am a mess-up. Since the day my brother died, I have been trying to fight the stereotype, but today, I've proven them right.

God, I can't think about what my father is going to say when he finds out I've been arrested. He will really think he has no sons left. It's preferable to thinking your only child left is sitting in jail, possibly for the rest of his life.

The elevator doors close, and then it's just me and Hayes in the elevator. Hayes presses the button for the third floor. He doesn't look at me, and I don't look at him. When the doors open, Hayes pushes me out in a stern and forceful way that is all business. I'm nothing to him, just like every other criminal he has arrested.

He leads me into the interrogation room where I know I will sit for the rest of the day. The FBI will then put me in the holding cell overnight and bring me back to the interrogation room in the morning. I'll go back and forth until they think they have gotten all they can from me. Then, I'll be sent to prison where I'll have no chance at escape, no chance at saving Kinsley.

Hayes removes the cuffs before leaving me alone in the room. I rub my sore wrists, just like I've seen the criminals who have been brought into this room before do.

I can't think about me though. All I can think about is

where Kinsley is and what she is doing. She must have found the letter. I searched everywhere in our room in the bed and breakfast and couldn't find it. I was stupid enough not to read it earlier, so I have no idea what it says, but it must have said enough of the truth to make Kinsley feel like she has to go set everything right.

I just don't know if it gave her a clue as to where she should go. If it did, I'm afraid it's going to send her to Mexico, to the one place in the world she shouldn't go. It isn't safe. And I can't do a damn thing about it.

The door opens, and my boss is standing there—well, my former boss. I'm sure, at the very least, I've been fired for my actions. He walks slowly over to the table. He sits down across from me, and I see a cup of water in his hand.

I smirk. I wasn't sure if he was going to be the good cop or the bad cop. I guess he is going with the good cop routine, which will make Hayes the bad cop. The idea of that makes me laugh.

Bisson pushes the water across the table to me. "It seems you have gotten yourself into quite a predicament, Byrne."

"Yes, sir," I say automatically before I realize all the niceties in the world won't help me now.

"I want to help you, Byrne. You are going to let me help you, aren't you?"

"I don't think you can help me."

He smiles. "I can. See, this whole thing boils down to one simple question and one simple answer. Do you want to be an FBI agent, or do you want to help a silly girl? If you want to be an FBI agent, you will answer anything I ask you, which is simple really. Where is the girl?"

"I don't know where she is. She lied to me, the same as she did to you."

Bisson narrows his eyes at me, trying to determine if I am lying or not.

I don't want to do it, but it might be my only chance at gaining his trust. So, I reach into the back pocket of my jeans and pull out the note Kinsley wrote. I hand it to him and then stare down at my hands while he reads the short letter.

On the surface, the letter makes it seem like I am nothing to her. At the heart of it though, it says how much she really loves me because she wouldn't have lied to me if she didn't love me. She thought she was giving me my life back and keeping me safe.

She's wrong though. I don't have a life without her. I don't care about being an FBI agent anymore, no matter how much it hurts to think that. I feel like I no longer care about my brother every time I think that, but it's the truth. I'm not meant to be an FBI agent. I suck at this job. All I care about now is keeping Kinsley safe.

"You don't know where she is?"

I shake my head. "No. I thought she was coming back here. I thought the same as you—that she was turning herself in."

In the back of my mind, I know where she is. I know what her father's note said without reading it—the truth.

Robert Felton loved his daughter above everything. That is the one thing I know to be true about that man. So, that note told her the truth.

I know exactly where she is—Cancún, Mexico, the last place I ever wanted her to go—and there is nothing I can do about it.

I look up at Bisson, who is intently staring at me. He's trying to determine if I am lying or not, but I know he can't read anything but my desperation for a girl I love but can't save.

He gets up from the table. "Think about it some more. Think long and hard about where she could be. Then, I'll be back."

I watch as he walks out the door, leaving me alone in the gloomy room. Its only goal is to make me feel so depressed that I tell them everything I know. I can't though.

Instead, I think about Kinsley. I think about her red lips and short locks that somehow embody the strength that now encompasses her. I miss the naive girl who was so innocent and sweet that she would do anything for her family. After she faces what I know is coming, there won't be a drop of that girl left. She won't survive if I can't find a way out of here.

3

KINSLEY

I feel the warm light shining into the room despite the dark shades. I open one eye and realize the shades don't close fully, allowing the sun to peek through the cracks. I sigh. So much for sleeping the day away.

I pull the white linen sheets over my head and roll over, but that lasts all of five minutes. When I can't fall back asleep, I get up. I grab a robe hanging in the closet and put it on over the tank top and underwear I slept in. I haven't bothered to buy any additional clothing, so I'm stuck with just two outfits and two pairs of underwear.

I walk over to the shades and pull them open before walking out onto my balcony. I take a deep breath, smelling the salty air that comes from being so close to the ocean. The waves are calm this morning, as calm as I feel even though I should be a wreck.

I don't know what time it is. I could walk back inside and see, but the time doesn't really matter. I know I can't go to the address in the middle of the day. I have to wait until darkness settles in. That means I have all day to enjoy the beach, the drinks, and the food. I have one last day to enjoy the beauty of the world before I experience how dark it truly can be.

I walk back inside and find the room service menu. My eyes immediately go to the pancakes, doughnuts, and muffins, but then I think of Killian. He wouldn't order any of that crap, especially not if he needed to feel strong and fearless later. I need my strength. I skim the menu, looking for something Killian has fed me, but I don't find anything. The healthiest item on the menu is an egg-white omelet with spinach and goat cheese. I order it and a coffee.

I walk into the bathroom and decide to take a quick shower to wash away all of my travels while I wait for my breakfast. I turn the hot water on and take off my robe and underwear. By the time I'm done undressing, steam has filled the large bathroom.

I step inside and am immediately filled with memories of the last shower I had with Killian. I suck in a breath as I remember his hands traveling across my smooth stomach before grabbing my breasts. As the water streams down my chest, I can practically feel his hands there, torturing me and turning me on with his touch until I'm panting hard with need.

I close my eyes and let my hands travel over my body. I massage my breast, doing my best to imitate Killian's strong touch that drives me wild. I let my hands slide down my stomach to my pussy.

I find my clit, just like he would, and I massage myself in torturous circles, slowly letting my body grow with lust, before I move my hand faster in tight circles.

I picture his strong smirk, his lips on my neck, his thick erection pressing up against me, begging for attention but not giving into his own needs until I'm satisfied first.

And then he whispers something dirty in my ear just as I come all over his hand. I come as I picture it.

I keep my eyes closed after I come, trying to keep Killian with me for as long as I can. But I know I have to open my eyes and let him go soon. I have to focus on what I need to do. I set him free. I can't bring him back into my mess of a life.

A knock on the door forces my eyes open and requires me to say good-bye to the Killian I brought back into my life through my dreams.

I turn the water off, despite the fact I didn't shampoo my hair or wash my body like I'd planned. I grab the towel and quickly dry off before putting the robe back on.

"Coming!" I yell toward the door as I exit the bathroom. I run my hand through my newly cut short locks before I open the door.

One of the hotel employees is standing with a cart of food. "Where would you like it?"

"On the balcony," I say.

I hold the door to my suite open while he carries a tray of food in. I then find my purse to pull out a couple of dollars.

"Gracias," I say, handing the tip to the man before he exits my room.

I walk out to the balcony and take a seat in one of the two chairs. It's hard, seeing an empty chair sitting right next to me. Killian should be here. No one comes to resorts like this alone. People only come here with their significant others or families.

I sigh and pull the lids off the two plates of food. A single tear falls down my cheek at the sight in front of me. One of the plates is the omelet with fruit on the side, like I ordered. And the other plate has an assortment of pastries I didn't order.

It's like Killian is saying it's okay to have a little sweetness with my healthy breakfast. It just makes it all the harder to do this without him. I have to though. I want him to be happy, and he would never be happy with me if it meant giving up his job with the FBI.

I pick up the plate with my omelet and then add a doughnut to it. I smile at the food that is a little bit of me and a little bit of Killian. It's perfect.

I spend most of the rest of the day eating on the balcony, napping, and looking at the calm ocean that brings me even more peace the longer I stare at it. I wish this were my life—just sitting on the beach, enjoying the warm weather without a care in the world. If I survive this, I'm going to spend at least a month on the beach. Even if I have no money after all this is over, I don't care. I'll find a way to just sit here until I forget every horrible thing my family did.

When the sun slowly begins moving closer to the horizon, I get up from my chair and head back inside. I find my new cell phone I bought when I first got here. It's a pay-as-you-go phone no one should be able to track. At least, I don't think anyone can track this number to me. I dial my grandfather's cell number and wait, but no one answers.

It was a long shot. I wasn't expecting him to answer. He wouldn't have known it was me. He doesn't know I'm here. I just hope he is here. I need to convince him I'm on his side, or my plan will never work.

I end the call and try calling Killian's cell. I'm not going to speak if he answers. I just want to hear his voice. I just need to know he is okay and back in the US, back with the FBI. I did everything I knew to do to make that possible. I just need to know my scheming didn't go to waste.

I wait though, but there is no answer. I try his number one more time, but there is still no answer. *Damn it!*

I need him. I need to know he is okay, that he is going to move on. Instead, I got no answers. Instead, I just have to hope he will find a good life without me. I expect the FBI will continue the investigation, but I don't expect him to come running in here, like he would have before. He thinks I hate him. He wouldn't go out of his way to help someone he hates. I gave up on us. I just hope my words were strong enough he won't come after me, not beyond what his job requires anyway.

I walk back outside and watch the sunset. It's beautiful here. I could just stay here. No one would find me, not for a long time anyway. I would be safe here, but the world wouldn't be. Not as long as my family is out there, smuggling and killing.

I walk back in and put on the same clothes I wore the last night I had with Killian. I grab my purse with my cell phone and leave the rest of my belongings. I won't need them, not where I'm going.

I head downstairs. I try my best to soak in the beautiful modern lobby full of color and life, but I can't. I'm too focused on my mission to enjoy the last beautiful thing I might ever see.

I walk outside the hotel into the muggy air and dark sky that is getting darker by the second. The streets are still busy with people—some heading in from the beach, others just beginning to go out for a night of partying. I envy them, all of them—the families, the couples, the kids. I would easily trade my life for any of theirs.

I walk three blocks to a shopping mall I saw when the cab dropped me off at the hotel. I duck inside the first store. I don't know why, but I feel like I have to change. I can't wear the torn jeans and ratty shirt. I have to make a good first impression. I have to come off as strong and independent if I want them to believe me, and I won't be either of those things if I feel weak or if I'm thinking about Killian.

I walk up and down the racks of clothes. There are several things that would do, but I don't pick any of them up. I realize I'm stalling. I know this is the last step before I call a cab and walk into what is most likely going to be a suicide mission.

So, I force myself to pick up the next suitable outfit—a pair of black leather pants and a black halter top that will make my boobs look good.

I take them into the dressing room and slowly strip out of my jeans and T-shirt. I take my bra off and then slip on the pants and halter top. I was right. I look good in this. I'm lucky my body type looks good in most anything since designers make clothes with my body type in mind.

My ass looks good stuck in the tight pants, and just enough of my nipples is pushing against the thin fabric to make any man who looks at me melt in my hands.

I fluff my hair, pull my red lipstick out of my purse and apply it. I look hot and strong. It's the best I will be able to do. All I need now are some heels.

I gather up my clothes and head back out to find some heels. I easily find some and then check out, paying with cash. I'm still carrying my old clothes when I leave the store. I hold the clothes up to my nose and take a deep breath. I can still smell Killian's scent on them—a mix of expensive cologne and sweat I couldn't mistake for anyone but Killian. It's the last thing I have of him, but I have to let it go.

So, I walk over to the nearest trash can and reluctantly toss the clothes into the bin. And then I walk away before I change my mind and dig the clothes out of the trash. Before I change my mind and put Killian in danger.

I pull my phone out to call a cab. I'm surprised my hands aren't shaking as I dial the number. I expect to have butterflies swarming around in my stomach, but there are none. Whatever happens, I know I'm doing the right thing.

Ten minutes pass before the cab pulls up, and I climb inside.

"*Adónde?*" The cab driver looks to be in his early forties.

I pull up the address I have saved on my phone and hand it to him.

"Here," I say, pointing to the screen, knowing my Spanish isn't good enough to communicate where I need to go. And I don't know if his English is good enough for me to communicate with him either.

The man immediately begins shaking his head. He pushes the phone back into my hands. "No, no, no, *señorita*. I can't take you there. No safe."

I frown at him. "I have to go here."

"No. You go there, you never come back."

I sigh. I know the man is right, but I don't have a choice. I need him to take me there. I dig in my purse and pull out enough money to triple what the fare will be.

I hand the money to the man. "Take me there."

He shakes his head again. "No, no." He shoves the money back into my hands. "Stay at one of these hotels. Whatever your troubles, the hotels will fix them. Not that place. That place only brings pain."

I don't know how I'm going to get through to this man, but if he knows so much about this place, there is a good chance all the cab drivers know about it, and none will take me.

"*Señor*, please. I have to go there. My family has done

some bad things there. I don't believe anyone will hurt me. Not if they know who I am. My name is Kinsley Felton, and I have to make things right."

When I say my last name, I watch as his eyes widen with fear, and it rips through my heart. I didn't think we were bad people. I thought we were a good business family. Maybe that's what we are known for in the US, but here, it is clear we are known as vile, vicious people who deserve to die for what we have done.

He begins driving and doesn't say another word. I stare out the window and watch as the sky grows from dark to complete blackness. I watch the pretty lights of the hotels disappear as we drive farther and farther away from the tourist area and into the heart of the city.

The city seems nice, just like any other city I have ever been in, but then we turn, and my worst fears come true. We drive into what looks to be an abandoned part of the city, except I know it is anything but abandoned. It is full of a dark evil I never imagined existed.

The cab driver slows as we grow closer to our destination. His eyes glance into the rearview mirror, showing sorrow, pain, and hatred for me and for what my family has done to these people and this town.

He stops outside the worst building of them all. It's tall and dark and looks completely uninhabitable. The door is barely hanging on the hinges. The windows are mostly boarded up. The roof looks like it could collapse at any second.

I get chills just from looking at it. This is where my father, my grandfather, and my great-grandfather would come to do unthinkable things. This is where they came, so this is where I shall go.

I hand the money back to the cab driver, but he shakes

his head. He doesn't look at me. Instead, his eyes are focused on the door in front of us. A door I will soon enter and might never return from.

"Please, take it," I say, my voice strong.

"No, *señorita*. I can't take your money."

I sigh, but I leave the money in the backseat. Surely, he will take the money after I leave.

I slowly get out of the car. My feet in heels are unstable while walking on the gravel, but I walk steadily anyway toward the door, my destiny.

I think about my father. I hate him. I hate him for what he did. I hate him for writing me the letter I left in the hotel room. I couldn't bring it with me.

He supposedly wrote the letter to protect me, to keep me safe. He wrote it to ask for forgiveness.

It's all bullshit. He didn't write the letter to protect me. He wrote the letter because he knew I was the only one who could put a stop to everything. And he knew if he told me not to go, I would. He wrote it because he thought I could save him from his sins. He was right.

I take a step forward and then another and another. My anger overtakes any fear and keeps it buried deep inside me.

I glance up and only see the moonlight shining down on me. The cab driver drove away the second my feet hit the ground. I'm all alone.

I walk up to the abandoned building. I don't have to do this. It's not my responsibility to put an end to this. I don't even know if I can put an end to this. I don't even have a very good plan. My plan is based on convincing everyone I want to follow in my family's footsteps. Then, I'll either convince my grandfather to put an end to it or call the police once I've infiltrated them, know who all the players are, and have evidence against them. It's a terrible plan, but it's all I have. And I'm not turning back now.

I walk to the door and press my ear against it, trying to hear anything inside. I hear nothing but silence. *Is anyone even here? Could I be wrong? Could this address be an old one?* It might be too late. They might have already moved on to a new address I might never be able to find.

I try to decide if I should knock or just open the door and head in. Neither seems like a good option, but I decide it is better to be invited in than to walk around a dark building until someone finds me.

I just need to tell them my name. As soon as I do, they will have to listen. I don't know who is the boss in all of this, my family or someone else, but I do know if they want to continue working with my family, they will have to hear me out.

So, I move my ear from the door and force my hand to form a fist. Then, I knock as loudly as I can against the wooden door. I wince when the sound echoes in the alleyway. I glance behind myself to see whom I might have pissed off, but I don't hear a sound, and I don't see anyone. I turn back to the door and don't hear any movement inside.

I wait a few minutes and try knocking again.

Nothing.

Damn it!

I was wrong. I'm out of clues. I'm at a dead end. If they aren't here, I have no idea where they are. I have no idea where to find them. Everything I just did was for nothing.

I turn and walk away from the door while digging in my purse to pull out my cell phone. Now, I have to convince a cab driver to pick me up here. *Yeah, that's going to happen.* I glance down at my heels that now look like a terrible choice now that I have to walk to a safer area before I can get a ride back to my hotel.

"Don't move," a deep voice says.

My heart skips a beat at the sound. I drop my purse. *Shit.*

I steady my breathing and open my mouth to speak. "I'm—"

"Shut up, bitch," the man says as he presses a gun into my back.

I close my eyes. I'm going to die before I even had a chance to speak.

I gather myself and try again though because I know it is my only chance at surviving long enough to get inside. "I'm Kins—"

"I said, shut up!"

That's when I feel something hard come into contact with my head. My last thought is of Killian and his beautiful grin that is only for me. How I yearn to see it just one more time, but now, I never will.

4

KILLIAN

"Breakfast!" the officer yells as the door to the cell opens.

I don't move though. Instead, I close my eyes and turn over in bed. I've been in this jail for three days now. And, for three days, I've barely existed. I haven't eaten. I haven't showered. I haven't shaved. I haven't watched TV or read. And I haven't heard anything from anyone.

The only time I even seem alive is in the afternoon when I get an hour to make as many phone calls as I want. And, even though I know my calls are being monitored, it hasn't stopped me from trying to call Kinsley and her damn grandfather who got us both into this mess. It hasn't stopped me from calling my parents or Hayes. I've tried them all, but none of them answer. None of them give me any answers or peace.

So, when my time is up, I slump back to my bed and spend most of the day thinking.

I think about how the hell I'm going to get out of here. How the hell am I going to fulfill my promise to Robert Felton if I'm in here? How the hell am I going to protect Kinsley? I can't lose another person I love because I was stupid or too weak to save them. I won't survive. If Kinsley dies, even working for the FBI won't bring me any comfort or purpose in my life, not that they will take me back.

I just don't want to keep living if she is dead. I've already thought about ways to end my life in here if she dies. There are so many ways. It would almost be too easy. There's hanging. I could get into a brawl with one of the gangs. They would easily seek their revenge on me. I could overdose on drugs. I could slit my wrists with a razor. Or I could starve myself to death. I have so many choices.

I realize now what jail does to people. I've been here for only three days, and I'm already choosing death over living in here. Just three days without her. That's all I can bear.

I shouldn't be thinking about death. I should be thinking about how to get out of here and how to save her. But the truth is, even if I find a way out of here, even if the FBI lets me go today, there is a good chance she is already dead.

I grab my head as the painful thoughts overtake it, bringing such sharp pain that it is almost impossible to tolerate. I try to wait for the torment to disappear again, like it always does, but each time I think about her, it takes my brain longer and longer to push out the pain. I can't keep living like this much longer.

She's dead. I know it. She's dead, and I will be, too, as soon as someone confirms it. I'll be gone.

I just don't know when or if I'll ever find out the truth. I haven't even been told how long I will be in here. I don't know if I will have to face a trial or if the FBI are just going to use some national security law to keep me locked away. I know nothing, so I choose to do nothing but sleep.

I've tried talking with the FBI. I've tried reasoning with them. I've tried to explain that Kinsley isn't guilty, that I'm not guilty, and that we have to save her because she isn't safe. They won't listen to anything. All they want to know is where she is so they can bring her in, but they don't understand that by moving in, it would let the criminals that work with Kinsley's family know the FBI is there, and they would kill her before the FBI had a chance to save her.

"Here," my roommate says, tossing some things onto my stomach.

I open my eyes, despite the pain I still feel in my head at the thought that Kinsley is most likely dead. If she went to Mexico, she's dead. Even if her grandfather is there, it won't matter.

I look at what the man threw me. A protein bar, a bag of Doritos, and a banana now lie on my stomach.

I sit up in my bed and look at my cellmate. I still haven't asked his name, despite sharing a cell with him for three days now. I run my hands through my hair, not understanding why he is giving me any of his food.

"The breakfast here is shit. Just tasteless oatmeal." He nods in my direction. "Eat. You'll need your strength if you are going to survive in here."

I unwrap the protein bar and take a bite. I know I can't turn down the food he paid for even if the food he's offering me isn't much better than what the jail serves. Who knows what he did to get this food in the first place.

The first drop of the protein bar hits my stomach, and my body roars to life. I feel the ache in my core for the first time since I've gotten here, and I feel each bite of food ease the pain. It just makes me eat faster. I finish the bar and quickly move on to the banana. And, when I'm finished with the banana, I tear into the Doritos despite the fact they have no real nutritional value. They might as well be little pieces of cardboard. But when I taste the first bite of the cheesy goodness, I forget about that. It tastes better than any vegetable or healthy piece of meat I've ever eaten.

"Thanks," I say with a mouthful of Doritos.

The man nods but doesn't say anything. He just sits in the chair across from my bed, waiting until I'm finished chewing. That's when I realize maybe I shouldn't have taken the food. He might think I owe him something for consuming his food.

"I'm Santino Marlow," the man says when I'm finished.

"Killian Byrne," I say, extending my hand.

The man just stares at me like he has no idea what I'm doing. I pull my hand back. *Fuck, I'm an idiot.*

"I'll pay you back for the food."

He smirks at me. "No need. That was nothing to me."

I nod.

I have no idea what this guy wants. He looks like a majority of the other men in here. Tattoos cover his muscular body. His head is shaved. He looks like he belongs in here. So unlike me. I stick out like a sore thumb in a place like this.

"It's not what you think," he says.

"What?"

"The reason I'm in here. I'm not a druggie. I don't sell drugs. I didn't steal shit. I'm not in a gang."

"Then, why are you here?" I ask, risking getting punched.

But hearing this guy's story might just be the distraction I need to get me through today. At the very least, it would reduce the pain I feel right now.

"I'm in here because of a girl."

My eyes widen.

"And I suspect it's the same reason you are in here."

I nod.

"The key to surviving without the girl you love is to talk about it. It will kill you if not. I tried to keep it buried inside. I thought, if anyone in here found out, they would think I was a pussy, and I'd get jumped. The opposite happened though. They understood because every guy in here has a girl at home. Everyone has a bitch they miss."

He pauses and takes a bite of an apple I didn't see he was holding in his hand.

"I'm in here because my girl disappeared. Vanished. Nobody knows where she is." He shakes his head. "They think I did it just because we fought. I didn't do it. I wouldn't lay a finger on her." He looks up at me. "The key to not thinking about her is to keep busy."

He stands and motions for me to follow. So I do.

"We have time in the yard this morning. You play ball?"

I shrug.

"Good."

I follow Santino out to the yard and find a concrete basketball court with two hoops that are barely standing upright. A dozen men or so are already involved in a game. One man shoots but misses the hoop entirely.

"Get out of there, Kenny," Santino says to a scrawny man that can't be much older than eighteen.

The man obediently walks off the court, like he's too afraid not to do exactly what he was told. I understand the feeling. Outside, I felt powerful and in control. In here, I have no powers. I barely even understand the rules.

"Who's this?" a man double my size says to Santino.

I'm not going to let Santino answer for me.

"Killian. Here to play," I say.

He glares at me. "Can you?"

I take the ball from his hand, and then I dribble and

shoot what should be a three-pointer. The ball goes in with ease.

I turn back to him. "I'll be taking Kenny's place."

I spend the next hour on the court. It feels good to be running and sweating again. Although I'm not the best player on the team, I pull my weight enough not to get treated like Kenny. My team easily wins.

Santino was right. Distraction is the best way to spend my time here. As long as I'm doing something, I'm not thinking about Kinsley. I'm not living in constant agony.

I grab a cup of water and take a seat at one of only two benches near the court.

Santino walks over and takes a seat next to me. "Tell me about your girl."

I sip on the water. "She's the same as your girl. She disappeared. The only difference is, I know where she is. I just can't tell the FBI. If I do, she will die." I take another sip of my water. "She might die anyway if I don't get out of here."

Santino nods, staring straight ahead, as he sips his water. "I might be able to help you with that," he says without looking at me.

"What? How?"

He shakes his head as a guard walks onto the court.

"Tomorrow," Santino says, getting up.

But I don't think I can wait till tomorrow. If he has a way out of here, even an illegal one, I need to take it now. I can't wait till tomorrow. Tomorrow, she could be dead.

The guard walks over to me. "Killian?"

"Yes."

"Come with me. You have a visitor."

I follow the guard even though I don't want to, not now that I have hope.

5
———

KINSLEY

I OPEN MY EYES, but it is still as dark as when my eyes were closed. I try to grab my pounding head with my right hand but find it handcuffed to something large and metal behind me. My left arm is free though, so I use it to massage my temple, trying to ease the pain. It helps a little, but I know I'm going to have a headache for weeks from where the man hit me in the head with the butt of his gun.

I try to look around the room to get a bearing on where I am or how long I was knocked out. I don't have a clue though. It could have been minutes, hours, or days. The room tells me nothing. There are no windows to let me know what time of day it is.

I shiver and move my arm away from my head, wrapping it around my body to try to warm myself up. I wish I had brought a jacket, but I never thought I would need one in the heart of summer in southern Mexico—that is, if I'm still in Mexico.

My heart rate increases at the thought, instantly warming me just a little. I could be anywhere. They could

35

have taken me anywhere. And, if I'm not in Mexico, then I'm completely and truly fucked.

My grandfather knew about the place in Mexico. Killian knew about the location. Somebody could have helped me if I needed them. But not now. Now, I'm on my own.

My eyes slowly begin adjusting to the darkness, and I start to make out a little bit of my surroundings. There is a door across from me—wood and sturdy. It couldn't be easily kicked in, like the main door to the building. The rest of the room is small with four walls and a wooden floor.

I'm attached to a heavy metal pipe. I test the strength of it, but I know there is no way my scrawny arms could bend it. I test the handcuffs, but I don't have a clue how to pick a lock or get them off. I'm stuck where I am, sitting on the wooden floor with one arm attached to the pipe that juts into the wall.

There are no windows. There is no other exit, other than the door. There is no way out for me. I'm entirely at these people's mercy until they decide what to do with me. Until they decide if I get to live or die. I swallow down those thoughts though. I can't think about them. I have to be strong.

I try to think of all the times I've been strong. None come to mind. All that comes to mind is when I've been weak, naive, and gullible. Even Killian said I was naive.

I shake my head. But he also thought I was strong and capable of running the company. He loves me. He wouldn't love someone he saw as just a meek, little girl. I've grown. He's helped me, and I've grown stronger than I ever imagined I could.

I can do this. I will survive this. I will put a stop to this.

A man's voice yells, followed by another man's even louder voice. Both are muffled, just beyond the doorway.

I startle at the sudden sound, as I got used to the silence. I strain my ears, trying to listen, but all I understand is the men are mad and arguing. I hope they aren't arguing over whether to let me live or die. I strain my ears trying to listen, but the voices quickly fade into the distance.

I try to close my eyes and sleep. Despite having been knocked out, I'm still exhausted, and my head is pounding. There is nothing else to do but sleep anyway. I move until I'm lying down on the hard floor and then force my eyes closed, despite the fear that I will never get the chance to open them again.

———

The door is thrown open, blinding me with light from the hallway and thrusting me from my dreamless sleep. The light just makes my head hurt worse.

"Eat," a deep voice says.

I hear two things drop in front of me.

The man immediately turns.

"Wait!"

The man doesn't listen. He keeps walking.

"Wait! You need to know, my name is Kinsley Felton."

The door closes though. He didn't hear me.

A tear rolls quickly down my cheek. I wipe it away with the back of my hand. I will not let my fear overtake me. Next time that door opens, I will shout my fucking name over and over until the message sinks in.

I look around the room again, but the darkness is too much. My eyes need time to adjust before I can see again.

I reach forward into the darkness, trying to feel what the man brought me. I feel a bowl and pull it to me. I feel around in the bowl but don't find any silverware. From what I can tell, it's rice and beans.

I scoop some into my hand and bring it to my mouth before I realize this might not be the best idea. It could be poisoned. I could die if I eat this. My stomach growls, letting me know it hasn't been fed in a long time. I could die if I don't eat it. And it doesn't make sense for them to poison me, not when a bullet is so much easier.

I force the food into my mouth, like an animal would. The food is cold, but despite the temperature, it tastes amazing. It's just beans and rice, like I suspected. I don't care though. It's food, and with each bite, I feel my strength coming back.

I quickly eat every morsel in the bowl. My stomach feels full and satisfied as the last drop of food goes down. That's when I realize how thirsty I am. I reach forward and find a bottle of water sitting next to where the bowl was. I unscrew the top of the bottle and gulp the whole thing down.

I glance around in the darkness. Now that I'm finished, I wish I had taken my time because there is nothing left to do but sleep or stare into the darkness while plotting all the ways I want to kill these men.

The door bursts open again, and from what I can tell, the same man from before walks to me.

I don't hesitate this time. "I'm Kinsley Felton! Kinsley Felton!" I repeat over and over. "I'm the daughter of Robert Felton. The granddaughter of Lee Felton. They sent me here."

The man bends down and releases me from the hand-cuff holding me in place. My immediate thought is to run, but I can't. I'm supposed to want to be here. I need them to trust me, not think I'm going to run away. I wouldn't make it far anyway—not in my heels, with my pounding headache, or with this man's strong hand holding my arm so hard I want to cry from the pain.

I don't though. I just keep repeating, "I'm Kinsley Felton." It's almost a battle cry against the pain now pulsing through my body.

"Shut up, bitch," the man says, hitting me hard on the head again.

I immediately shut my mouth as the room begins spinning. I don't know if I could chance saying another syllable. If he hits me on the head again, he could do some permanent damage, I'm sure.

The man begins walking, dragging me through the door, before I'm steady on my feet.

"Walk," the man says, shaking me like I'm purposely struggling to walk instead of doing my best to walk through the dizziness and headache.

I try to steady myself and keep up with his pace, but I can't. So, instead, I stumble as he drags me down the bright hallway. I try to glance around the hallway to figure out where the exits are. To figure out where I am. I look around the building that seems less broken on the inside than the outside, but I have no idea if I'm in the same building I knocked on.

The man turns left, heading down another hallway. I turn my attention to him. I need to study every person here. When the time comes to turn them over to the FBI or police, I need to know who is involved and what their jobs are. This man is tall. It's hard to tell how strong he is, but the grip on my arm tells me he has plenty of strength. His skin is whiter than mine, and his hair is blond and unkempt. Honestly, when I look at him, he looks like a typical American man in his jeans and T-shirt that fit a little tighter than they should.

We stop in front of a door that he knocks on calmly and steadily. It seems out of character for the man who seems to have no patience.

"Come in," a deep voice says.

The man holding on to me opens the door, pushes me in the room, and then steps in behind me.

"Sit down." A man sitting behind the desk in front of me points to the chair in the center of the room.

I quickly take a seat, thankful not to be standing in my dizzy state any longer. I glance around the room that is much larger than any other office I have been in before. At least a dozen men are standing against the walls, smirking, grinning, or glaring at me.

I try to remain calm and strong as I turn my attention back to the man behind the desk. He's tall, his skin is darker than mine, and his hair is almost as long, but it's his piercing, ruthless eyes that have me trapped. He's only wearing a dark T-shirt and jeans, nothing that says he has any authority here, but his eyes command the attention of the room. He walks around the desk and then leans against it while he curiously looks at me.

I open my mouth to speak, but then I think better of it, as the man who hit me before is still standing right behind me, and I can't take getting hit again.

"My name is Nacio Marlow. I run this organization you see here." He gestures to the men at his sides. "These are my men."

My eyes drift from side to side to the men who are intently listening to him while staring at me. Each one of them looks like he could kill me with just his bare hands.

"We have never had an uninvited guest here in the ten years we have been working from this location." His lips curl up into a psychotic-looking grin as he walks to me. He grabs my chin as he looks into my eyes. "So, what is a pretty girl like you doing here?"

This is my chance to tell him. To convince him I am on his side. To convince him I am a ruthless Felton, just like my father and grandfather before me. This is my chance to save myself, to keep myself breathing for another day, but instead of speaking, I freeze. I open my mouth to speak, but nothing comes out—not one word, not even a breath.

Nacio frowns and walks back to his desk. "Persuade her, Seth," Nacio says to the man standing behind me.

My eyes immediately close as I wait for another knockout hit that will leave me feeling like a vegetable when he is finished with me. It never comes though. Instead, I feel the end of a gun pushing into my temple. The feel of the cold metal pressed against my head is enough to knock me out of my frozen spell.

I take a deep breath. I have to play this right. I can't seem like a scared, naive girl begging for her freedom. I try to channel all of my inner Scarlett, my best friend that has all of the confidence in the world. I stare straight ahead at Nacio, ignoring the gun pressed against my head. "I suggest you have your goon remove the gun from my head."

Nacio cocks his head to one side with a smug grin on his face. "And why would I do that, sweetheart?"

"Because I'm Kinsley Felton, daughter of Robert Felton, granddaughter of Lee Felton. And, if you don't remove the gun from my head right now, I will make sure the Feltons never work with the Marlows ever again. I will make sure that we destroy the Marlows."

Nacio's eyes read fear for just a second, not long enough for his men to notice. Not long enough that I'm even really sure of what I just saw, but enough that I know the fear was there. His family fears mine.

I glare at him, my eyes focusing intently on his, even though I want to smile because I know I'm not going to die today. Today, I'm going to live. Today, I'm going to become the next one in charge. Today, I'm going to take over a smuggling ring.

But Nacio doesn't give the signal for Seth to lower his gun. The gun is just as firmly pressed against my head as it was a second ago.

And my fear returns.

I don't let it show though. I can't. If I do, I know I'll be dead.

A wry smile appears back on Nacio's lips. "Excellent. Now that we have found all of the Feltons that are left, it's time to kill them."

6

—————

KILLIAN

I DON'T KNOW who is going to be sitting across the table from me when the door opens to the visitation room. The guard guides me into the room. Hayes is standing in the corner, and I'm not surprised. Not at all. I didn't expect my family to travel out of Kansas. I don't have any other friends, other than Hayes. I'm not sure I'm allowed visitors even if I did. I think a small part of me was hoping it was Kinsley. Even if it had meant her going to jail, it would have meant she was still alive. Still safe for another day.

Hayes looks at me as I enter. His eyes are red and puffy, like he's been crying. His body looks worn down, almost broken. He's wearing his typical suit all FBI agents wear when not undercover. If I didn't know any better, I would think he just came from a funeral instead of the office.

"Who died?" I ask sarcastically as I sit down at the table.

Hayes doesn't sit. Instead, he looks out the small window for a second. "You can leave," he says to the guard.

"I have to stay, sir. It's protocol," the guard says.

Hayes pulls out his FBI badge. "I have classified FBI business I need to discuss. Leave," he says.

The guard frowns at Hayes. "At least let me handcuff him to the table."

"That won't be necessary. He will be leaving the jail in an hour or two anyway."

The guard hesitates for a second longer and then leaves.

"I'm leaving, huh? Found me innocent or taking me to a high-security prison? Or maybe you think you can get me to talk about Kinsley in exchange for my freedom?"

"Shut up, Byrne."

"Why am I here, Hayes?"

Hayes runs his hand through his hair and then takes a seat across from me. "Because you were right."

My eyes widen. "What do you mean, I was right? You found Kinsley? Her grandfather? What else do you know?"

"Yes, we found them. And we probably know about as much as you do now."

"Where are they? Is she safe? Do you have her in custody?"

Hayes looks down at his hands. He won't meet my eyes. And I know it's bad. They have her—the drug lords, the smugglers. The monsters have her. And the FBI is breaking me out, so we can go after them.

He finally glances back up at me, somberly, and I swear, I see a tear in his eye.

"She's dead, Byrne. They both are."

I fall back in my seat. My hands go to my hair, grabbing my pounding head. I can't process what he just said because she can't be dead. She can't be.

"She's not dead," I say.

"Killian..." Hayes never calls me by my first name, making me wince. "She's gone. We found her body this morning along with her grandfather's and mother's. Well, what's left of their bodies."

"Show me."

Hayes shakes his head. "I can't do that. You wouldn't be able to get that image out of your head if I showed you."

"Show me," I demand. "I need to see what they did to her. I need to see that she is actually gone to believe it."

Hayes reluctantly reaches into his pocket and pulls out his cell phone. He scrolls until he finds the picture and then slides the phone across the table to me. I pick it up.

I thought I could handle it. I've seen enough crime scene pictures of bodies that are more horrifying than this. But this rips me apart—seeing Kinsley, her grandfather, and her mother burned to pieces. They almost look unrecognizable, but I know it's Kinsley. In my heart, I knew they would kill them once they knew the FBI was investigating them. It gets too messy for them to keep Kinsley and her family alive. I just don't know who *them* is yet. But I plan to.

I can't hold it together any longer as tears streak down my face while I look at what is left of my beautiful princess.

"How did she..."

"Gunshot wound. She must have died instantly. They burned her body after she was already dead."

I know his words are supposed to comfort me. That she died instantly. That she wasn't in any pain. It doesn't comfort me. Nothing ever will again.

Nothing.

Tears fall faster now, and I wish Hayes wasn't here. I hate feeling weak in front of someone else, especially him, but as I glance up through my tears, I see he is almost just as torn apart by her death as I am. So, we both just cry across from each other. Not connecting or trying to comfort the other. But still sharing her death all the same.

Hayes stops crying. My tears stop long before I have come to terms with my grief. Still, when my tears dry up,

Hayes takes the time to talk. Like that is something I am capable of right now.

"I'm going to get you out of here."

Hayes waits for me to respond, but I can't. I don't care if I live the rest of my life in here or out there. It will feel like a prison to me either way.

"You can't work for the FBI again. They don't trust that you will follow their commands, which is all they care about. They think you'll go rogue again. In fact, they want to give you a security detail until we close the case and make sure you are safe. You can't go after them though. You would just get yourself killed, too. You have to let us handle it."

Hayes pauses to allow me time to promise him to let the FBI handle it. I won't promise him though.

"You should go home. Your family is worried about you. Even your father is worried."

I look at him now, not understanding. "My father?" I croak through my dry mouth.

He nods. "They are at the FBI office, waiting for you. Both of your parents are a mess. They just want you to come home. Your father said he couldn't lose another son."

I nod, although I can't believe my father still cares about me. I thought going to jail would effectively end our relationship, not be the thing that brought us back together.

"Killian, are you listening?"

"Yes."

"Good."

"I should go. I have a lot of paperwork to do to make sure you get out of here this afternoon."

I nod.

Hayes walks over, picks up his phone from the table, and pats me on the back. He doesn't say anything as he walks away. He doesn't have to. I can feel how sorry he is. And this isn't his fault.

This is my fault. I was the one who promised to protect her. I was the one who failed. I am the one who failed. She's dead, and it's my fault. Just like it's my fault my brother is dead. I bring death to everyone I meet. That is why the world would be better off if I were dead. Then, I couldn't cause anyone else to die. Then, those I loved would be safe.

The guard comes back into the room. He reaches down and grabs my shoulder, and I stand as he pulls me up. He puts the handcuffs back on and guides me back to my cell where my handcuffs are removed. Then, I'm left alone. Santino is gone.

Now is the time to kill myself. To get rid of the pain I know I'll never be able to escape from now that she is really gone.

But that's no longer what I want. Those thoughts are completely gone from my mind, despite the pain being worse than when my brother died. When he died, I wanted to kill myself, but I realized quickly that dying wouldn't help my brother. My penance was working for the FBI and taking over his role. But the real reason I took the FBI job was to go after his killers. I thought working for the FBI would let me get my revenge. It didn't.

Now, that's all I see. *Revenge.*

I have to go after her killers. I have to end their lives. It's the only way I will find peace. I can't protect her any longer, but I can protect the future Kinsleys of the world from a few less monsters.

My anger overtakes my body. I grab the bedding off my bunk and rip and tear it apart until it's a pile of shreds on the floor. I grab the pillow and rip it open, pulling the stuffing out and ripping it apart. I try to calm my anger so I won't start a fight with someone while I'm still in jail. If I do that, I might never get out. Or I might end up killing an innocent man.

My blood is pumping fast and warm through my veins as I grab Santino's bedding as well. He might kill me for this, but I don't care. I don't think. I tear his bedding to pieces, just like mine. The fabric so easily bends to my will. Just like the men who hurt Kinsley will as soon as I find them. They will be wishing they were dead pieces on the floor by the time I am done with them. Because death is not something I will give them, not until they have experienced every pain known to man. Because that is the pain Kinsley experienced. That is the torture I am going to face every day until I die.

"She was yours," Santino says as he leans against the door to our cell.

I narrow my eyes as I toss the last piece of stuffing onto the floor. "Who?"

"The girl who is all over TV. The daughter of the billionaire casino owner. She was your girl."

"Yes."

I glance past him, and that's when I see the TV showing nonstop coverage of Kinsley, her grandfather, and her mother. It will be all over the news for weeks. A beautiful girl like Kinsley will be hard for the news crews to just drop the story without answers and outrage from their viewers.

I watch Scarlett in tears on the TV. And I see that the news outlet even have Kinsley's ex-boyfriends, Eli and Tristan, coming on next. They'll have any person who ever spoke to her on. Every grocer, mailman, and neighbor who ever spoke to her will come on and speak. It brings me some comfort to know she won't easily be forgotten. Even though she's dead, she won't fall from everyone's memory. She will

live on. That's why I have to live—to keep her memory alive when the media has moved on to the next scandal.

"Still want a way outta here?" Santino asks.

I incredulously stare at him. I have a way out now. A way out where I can see my family. Where I can find out what the FBI knows about what happened to Kinsley even if they won't let me stay on. A way where I will be watched like a hawk and have no chance at ever getting my revenge.

But, if I go with Santino, I will be a fugitive. The second the FBI finds me, they will send me back to jail. But, if I get my way and end the men who killed Kinsley, I will be a fugitive anyway. Either way, I will end up back in this jail—no, in prison for the rest of my life. At least, if I kill them, my heart will be able to rest.

I look at Santino. I have no idea why he is offering to help me or what payment I will have to pay for my freedom. I don't even know if he can get me out of here. But I know I have to take the chance.

"Yes, get me out of here."

A slow grin curls up his face. "Wait here," he says before he vanishes.

I look at the mess I've made and begin tossing the torn sheets back onto the bunk beds. If any of the guards see this, they will think something is up and reprimand us. I can't take the chance, not when I'm so close to freedom and revenge.

I toss the last piece of stuffing back onto the bed when Santino returns.

"Let's go."

I follow him out of our cell, but I wish I knew what the plan was instead of just blindly following him. Now, I am completely at his mercy, and I have no idea who else might be involved in the plan.

As we near the edge of the main room where we all hang out, a fight breaks out across the hall.

"Shit," I say under my breath. Now, we will never get out of here. The place will go into lockdown for the rest of the day, and we won't get a chance again because Hayes will be getting me out.

But, when I look at Santino, he isn't fazed at all. It's part of the plan, I realize. But who would be willing to pose a fake fight and possibly be in here for longer just to help two other men escape? It makes no sense.

Santino ducks inside the kitchen, and I do the same. The kitchen is crazy with people pushing carts of food in and out of the building. It's shipment day. The one day a week when the food for the whole jail is brought into the building, and everyone is busy pushing carts in and out as fast as they can. Prisoners and guards and chefs are all busy with moving things around. No one is paying us any attention.

Santino walks to the far side where a large empty crate sits, ready to be moved out of the building.

He opens the door to the large crate. "Get in."

I climb in without a word, and Santino climbs in right after me. We don't say a word as he closes the lid, and darkness covers us.

We both sit in the darkness, not moving, not speaking, barely breathing, for fear we will be found. Eventually, the cart starts moving. We are rolled out of the building and up a ramp to what I assume is a truck. We stop for a while, and then I hear the truck moving.

We drive for hours. We drive so long that the tears at losing Kinsley come back. I let them out, knowing Santino can't see me in the darkness.

The truck eventually comes to a stop. To my surprise,

Santino climbs out. He doesn't wait until whatever man driving the truck is gone.

I climb out after him.

He lifts the door to the back of the truck and jumps out. I follow.

"Thanks, man. I owe you one," I say.

Santino stops and looks at me. "I was hoping you would say that. Because I'm supposed to deliver you to my brother."

Fuck, I think as I realize where I know Santino from. It's the last thing I think before losing consciousness.

7

KINSLEY

FUCK. I was wrong. They are going to kill me.

I close my eyes and wait for the trigger to be pulled. At least the pain in my head will be gone when I'm dead. And at least Killian will be safe.

I wait one...two...three seconds, but nothing happens. The trigger isn't pulled, and the gun isn't lowered.

Maybe I'm already dead? Maybe this is an illusion?

I open my eyes, expecting to be floating above my body that must be broken and bloody on the floor. Instead, I'm sitting in the same position. I glance up at Nacio, who is grinning wildly at me. He's won, and he knows it. I gave him a drop of fear, and he ignited it. He had no intention of killing me—at least, not yet—but he's just proven he has the upper hand here. Not me.

He laughs, and then all the men in the room are laughing along with him. My cheeks flush in embarrassment.

I push the gun away from my head and stand, finally able to breathe again. I walk over to Nacio with a tight glare on my face, showing I don't appreciate his games. I can't let him win this fight, not when my life and the lives of those I love are on the line.

He stops laughing and smugly looks up at me.

"I didn't come here to play games. I came here to take my father's place in the company."

Nacio grabs the neck of my shirt and jerks me forward until my face is inches from his. His grip around my shirt tightens, making it hard for me to breathe.

"I don't play games either. Don't threaten my life, and I won't threaten yours."

He releases me, and I can breathe again. My heartbeat has just gone through a roller coaster of ups and downs in a matter of minutes, and I'm not sure it can survive much more without suffering a heart attack. It's no wonder my dad died from a heart attack if he had to deal with people like this on a daily basis.

He begins walking to the door before he turns and looks me up and down. His eyes lust over the curves of my chest then ass in the tight clothing. "Follow me, princess." His voice is harsh.

I don't react when he says, princess. At least I do everything in my power not to react when I want to cringe in disgust. I don't want it to become his pet name for me.

I walk toward him as confidently as I can in my heels as I toss my grungy hair behind my shoulders. I feel every man's eyes in the room on my ass. If it weren't for my time modeling, I would be completely disgusted by the thought. Now though, I know it's my greatest power to control these men, and I'm going to use it.

I pause for just a second when I reach Nacio. "It's Kinsley. Not princess. Not sweetheart. Not baby. I am none of those things to you."

I strut past him out the door and into the hallway. I don't

wait for him. I just keep walking down the hallway, hoping I will be able to find my grandfather or find out more information about the operation.

I hear Nacio yell at his men to get back to packing.

And then he is right at my side. "Slow down, sweetheart," he says in his slick voice.

I roll my eyes at his childish games. "I thought we weren't playing games with each other."

His grin widens until it covers his face. It's a grin that might usually make my knees weak if I didn't know what kind of monster lies beneath the wicked smirk. And if my heart didn't still long for another grin. A grin that puts Nacio's grin to shame. A grin that only I cause on Killian's face. Not like Nacio's that is probably given out to every girl he sees.

Just thinking about Killian makes me want to run out the door and forget why I even came here, but I can't.

"Not games, but if we are going to work together, I think we should be on friendlier terms than first names, sweetheart."

Nacio touches my neck, and I freeze. He's flirting. He's known me all of five minutes, and he's already flirting. He doesn't even know if he can trust me yet. I suck in a breath, trying to decide if I should let him flirt or if I should flirt back. It might make it easier to get him to tell me everything, to get him to trust me. But, as his slimly hand strokes my neck, I know I can't. I can't fake attraction for him. I'm not a good enough actress. So, instead, I go for controlling bitch.

I slap his face as hard as I can. I watch as his face turns away from me, and his hand goes from my neck to his cheek. He turns back to me. But his face doesn't wear a surprised look. Instead, he's grinning like he was expecting that reaction all along, and somehow, being hit makes him more attracted to me.

"I think you and I will get along well, sweetheart."

"Show me around, and take me to my grandfather. And don't touch me again without asking, or I will cut your balls off in your sleep."

His grin widens. "This way, sweetheart."

I sigh. At least he decided to settle on sweetheart instead of princess. It still sounds disgusting falling from his twisted lips, but at least he doesn't get to taint the term that is Killian's and my father's name for me. At least I can still have that.

"These rooms serve as our offices. At least the men who are high enough to need an office and aren't just doing the grunt work."

"Should I be introduced to the other men in charge?"

Nacio stops walking and sternly looks at me. "No, I'm in charge. You've already met my right hand, Seth. And my younger brother will be here soon. Other than that, you don't need to worry about getting to know the other men."

I nod although I don't like it. I need to know the name of every man who has any power in this company. If not, when I call the police to move in, some of the men could run and start this over again somewhere else. I won't let that happen.

"Still, if I'm going to be running the company, don't you think I should know all the names of our employees?"

He shrugs. "Not really. I don't even know most of their names. The less we know about each other, the better. Most don't stay long anyway."

I pause at a cracked door as chills roll through my body. I feel a connection to this room. I don't ask Nacio for permission as I push the door open. He doesn't say anything as I walk into the large office. I switch the light on and watch as it flickers to life.

A desk sits across the way, just like in Nacio's office. Several chairs sit in front of it. I look to my left and find a nice leather couch against that wall. I hesitantly walk over to the desk, afraid of what I'm going to find, as every nerve in my body ignites.

I pause when I get to the desk and run my hand along the solid wood surface. A computer and two picture frames are all that sit on the desk. I reach out and touch one of the frames. I know whose office this used to belong to before I glance at the photo.

I turn the frame so I can see the photo of me riding on my father's shoulders. It is the same frame sitting in my father's office in the casino in Las Vegas.

This office was my father's. I immediately want to scream and cry. I hate that my father has an office in such an awful place. I want to destroy this office, just like I did to his office in Las Vegas. I can't though, not without letting Nacio know I hate my father instead of love him.

Nacio puts a hand on my shoulder in what is meant to be a comforting manner, but it just creeps me out. I haven't even seen the man do anything horrible yet, but it still gives me the creeps.

"Your father was a good man. He's been missed. I hope you can fill his place. I would hate to lose you, too."

I suck in a breath at his threat. "You won't be disappointed."

"Good."

"Will this be my office now?"

"No."

He walks out the door without another word, leaving

me confused. I follow him out and try to keep pace as he picks up speed until we reach the staircase.

"Where will my office be?"

He shakes his head. "You haven't earned an office yet. Nobody gets to the top without doing the grunt work first. Nobody, not even if they have the last name Felton."

He begins up the stairs two at a time, and I follow at a more leisurely pace, not liking what he just said.

"Where is my grandfather?"

"He's not here."

I narrow my eyes. "What do you mean? Where else would he be? He's not in Las Vegas."

"They are at a different location."

"They?" I stop in my tracks, wondering if my father isn't really dead.

"Your grandfather and mother."

I try not to react, but I know my eyes widen just a little. I didn't think my mother was involved. I thought she might have been the most moral person in our family. But nothing truly surprises me anymore about my family. My father and grandfather are rotten, horrible, vile people. So, why not my mother, too?

I nod, as if I remember now. "And where is the other location?"

He shakes his head. "You haven't earned that information yet."

I frown.

Nacio turns from me and begins walking again. "These are the men's barracks." He gestures to the rooms on either side.

"We haven't had a girl stay with us in quite a while." He stops and smirks. "Well, not one we didn't plan on torturing, raping, or killing."

I frown in horror. *God, I'm not going to be able to keep this up.* He is going to find out that I'm not up for this. That I'm only here to destroy him. He doesn't seem to notice my reaction. Instead, he turns back and walks to the door on the far end.

"But since we have already started moving several of our men to the other location, this room is empty. It's yours while you are here."

The door is already open, so I step inside the large room that contains six sets of bunk beds. They don't appear to have been occupied for a while. But there is a stench that hovers about the room. The sheets on the beds don't look like they have ever been laundered, and dirt and mud cover the floor. At least I will have my own room though. At least I won't have to worry about one of the men getting too friendly in the middle of the night. I doubt Nacio sleeps in anything this bad. From the looks of him, he is accustomed to nicer things.

"If it isn't up to your standards, you can always sleep in my bed, sweetheart."

I shudder at that thought. "I'll make do."

"Good. Now, let's get down to business."

I nod. The sooner we get down to business, the sooner I'll be done.

He gestures for me to follow him, and we begin walking again.

"As you probably already know, our operation has been compromised. The FBI found out about the money laundering, and there is a good chance they know about our operation as well."

I nod.

"We are working to put a stop to the FBI coming after us."

"How?"

He ignores me and walks back to the staircase. He begins walking higher and higher up the stairs until I'm sure we can't safely climb any higher in this rickety building. He leads me down another dark hallway that has men standing outside each of the doors.

"We need to fake your deaths."

I twist my hair as we walk. I hate this hallway. Chills inch over my body with every step we take. I don't understand why, but I know something dark is here. Something that brings more pain than I can even understand.

"Why?" I ask, turning my attention from the hallway and back to Nacio.

"So the FBI will stop investigating. We will give them bodies. We will lead them to this place where they will catch some lowlifes we have left behind, who they'll think were in charge. But then it will lead to a dead end. Meanwhile, we will be safe to move our operations elsewhere."

My mind is spinning as he talks. I'm trying to understand why we need to fake our deaths. "How is it even possible? Even if we give them bodies, won't they know with DNA testing those bodies aren't us?"

Nacio sighs, like he has been explaining something very simple to a three-year-old. "No."

He turns his attention away from me. The man guarding the door we have stopped outside of moves to the side as Nacio grabs ahold of the doorknob.

Everything inside of me is screaming not to go through that door. To run. To go anywhere but here.

Instead, I watch as Nacio pushes the door open, and I force my legs to walk in after him.

The first thing I notice is the stench. It's not the same as the one I smelled in what will be my room for the next few nights. This room smells worse, if that is possible. It smells of urine, vomit, and...blood.

It's a dark, small room, much like the room I was held in earlier. It just makes me even more nervous.

Nacio stops a step or two inside the room. I stop just behind him, too scared to look around him, at what I'm sure is on the other side of him.

Nacio looks from the floor to me and then back to the floor. "Yes, you will do perfectly," he says to the floor.

He looks back at me, and I can see it. I can see excitement and lust in his eyes. I don't understand what has gotten him so excited, and I have to know. I have to understand what I'm really dealing with.

I take a step forward and to the side so I can see what Nacio was looking at. My body must turn white at the sight. My hands are cold and clammy. My heart stops beating at the sight that proves such evil exists. Evil I didn't think could ever exist, not even in the darkest corners of hell.

The sight before me is not something I ever imagined seeing.

A woman lies naked on the floor—or what is left of a woman. She doesn't try to cover her nakedness when she sees that other people are here, looking at her. Instead, she just lies on the ground with emptiness in her eyes.

One of her arms is tied to a post in the corner of the room, but I don't see the use in tying her up. She looks far too weak to even lift her head, let alone try to break out of this place.

Her body is thin, far too thin, with bruises and blood covering most of her body. From the amount of blood and bruises covering her, I suspect at least her ribs and one of her arms are broken. Her hair is dirty, but I guess it was a beautiful shade of blonde at one time.

I stare into her eyes, hoping I can give her hope if I can get her to look at me. She doesn't look at me though. I'm not even sure if she notices I am here. Instead, her blue eyes are glazed over to the point I'm not sure if she is really even here.

Nacio turns to me. "Ready for your first test?"

Alarmed, I look at him. I don't know what he is going to want me to do to this woman, but I can't hurt her. She's so broken anyway.

I open my mouth to tell him that when I see a dark piece of metal in his hand. He lifts the gun until it's pointing at the girl, and he pulls the trigger.

8
————

KINSLEY

I STARE at the woman who now has blood pooling from her head. It's an image I will never get out of my head for as long as I live. She will forever haunt me.

I don't remember what I did when he pulled the trigger. Did I scream? Or freeze? Or cry?

I don't know as my feet follow his down the hallway that holds more people. Any of whom could be killed in an instant. On a whim. Just because Nacio wants them dead.

I hate myself for not doing something to stop him. To save her. I should have realized why he brought me to that room. To kill a woman who looked like me, so he could leave her for the FBI to find. I should have known. I should have stopped him.

My only solace is maybe that is what the woman wanted. Maybe she was ready to die. Maybe he put her out of her misery. She was beyond saving. But, even if that were true, it wouldn't make my part in all of this any better. I could have stopped him, and I didn't. I might as well have pulled the trigger myself.

I continue silently following Nacio until we reach his

office. I watch his body bubble with the excitement from a kill. I watch him crack his neck when he reaches the door of his office, as if killing helped to release whatever tension he was feeling.

I hate him.

I should kill him.

I can't though. There is no way I could kill anyone, not even him. I'm too weak to handle that. But I already did, and the thought creeps into my head. I didn't pull the trigger, but I let that girl get killed. I didn't even know her name. I will never know her story, and now, she's just gone, and her family will never know what happened to her.

He walks into his office and picks up a cell phone from his desk. He dials a number and waits. He's not looking at me. He must have forgotten I'm even here.

"I need you to go up to room eight. Take the body and prepare it with the others to be dropped off at the location." He pauses and listens to whoever is on the other end of the call. "No! I need it done within the hour."

He pauses again as he turns. He sees me, remembering I am still here.

"Just get it done." He puts the phone down.

"Sit," he says to me.

I look at the chair in the center of the room. The chair I sat on with a gun pointed at my head. There is no way I'm sitting in that chair again. Instead, I pull a chair from against the wall up to his desk and take a seat. He takes a seat in his expensive-looking large leather desk chair across from me.

He stares, studying me. I try to remain as blank as possible. I know, if I don't, he is going to put a bullet in my head, just like he did that girl.

"You didn't react how I thought you would."

I try to force a smile onto my lips, but it is no use. I don't think I'll ever find a reason to smile again. "How did you think I would react?"

"I thought you would scream. I thought you would cry. Or I thought you would pass out from the shock. I didn't expect you to react so..."

"So?"

"So unfazed by it all. Like you knew it had to be done and just accepted it."

I tuck my hair behind my ear. "I'm not the naive girl you think I am. My father taught me to be stronger than that." None of the words leaving my mouth are true.

I don't know how he's drawn the conclusion he has. I am anything but unfazed. I'm a mess. I'm very fazed, but I can't let him know that.

He cocks his head to the side, like that is going to make a difference in how I look, and he studies me for further clues.

"The first kill I saw was when I was twelve."

My eyes widen. "Why so young?"

"My father began grooming my brother and me to take over when I was ten. He thought that was a good age to get started." He chuckles. "I didn't have a clue what was happening when I was ten. I was a punk who thought it was cool, smuggling drugs and things that gave us lots of money to have the best cars and the best houses. I didn't understand, not until I was twelve."

I watch his eyes glaze over as he goes back to wherever he was that day.

"It was a building, much like this one, that we were operating from at the time. I was being a smug punk, like always. A new guy, who was working for us, came in, and I harassed him to no end even though he had already been punished and was barely clinging on to life. Told him he had to do whatever I said because I was the boss's son. My father wasn't in the office that day. Your father was the one watching over me. He saw me harassing this man.

I had no idea why this man was on the verge of death. All I knew was that he had to do whatever I said, or I'd get to kick him. It was fun. It was a game to me. I didn't understand I was messing with someone's life.

"Your father, he couldn't stand it any longer. He took his gun out right in front of me and shot the man square in the head. I cried at the sight of the lifeless man lying on the floor."

I raise my eyebrows at him.

"I was twelve, so, yeah, I fucking cried like a baby. I didn't understand why your father had killed the man. When I finally settled down, he told me the work we did wasn't a game. It wasn't fun. We took from people's lives in order to better our own, and the sacrifice of those who had to die along the way deserved respect. That if I wanted to be the boss, I would have to face death on a daily basis, and until I was ready for that, I shouldn't order people around. That day, I stopped being a punk and became a man."

Tears stain my face. I can't hold them back. Nacio can just think that seeing someone die right in front of me is finally catching up to me. Or that I'm crying over missing my father instead of crying over the man my father was.

"I guess he prepared both of us to take over the roles we would one day have to do here. It was just in different ways. He showed me the truth while he protected you for as long as he could."

To my surprise, he hands me a tissue. I take it and wipe my eyes.

"It gets easier, watching it happen. It gets better and

better until you begin to find death as beautiful and enjoyable as life. And then, after the first time you kill, it gets hard again. And then so, so much fucking better."

I can't listen to his words. His words suck. I can't imagine watching someone die getting any better. I will always think of it as horrible. I don't want killing someone to get any better. It should never get better.

"I have some more arrangements to make. You can head to the first floor and grab some dinner."

I stand, ready to get as far away from Nacio as possible.

I make it to the door before he speaks again, "The first test isn't over. You've done well so far. Don't fuck it up."

I don't give him a response. I just turn from the door. I don't know what he means, that my first test isn't over. I know he doesn't trust me. But I don't know what he expects me to do.

Run. He expects me to run. That is my first instinct as soon as I leave his office. No one is here. No one is watching me. I could run. I could run away. I could go to the police and tell them where the location is and hopefully put an end to as much as possible.

But, if I ran, the next location would be safe. My grandfather wouldn't have to pay for what he did. My mother wouldn't have to pay. Nacio's brother and all of the men who have already moved wouldn't pay. And all the people at the next location wouldn't be safe. I can't run.

I glance to the corner of the hallway and see a security camera sitting in the corner. I couldn't run even if I wanted to. There is no way they would let me. I would end up dead. Just like the girl.

I catch my breath and then begin making my way downstairs. I'm surprised by how few people are moving around the building. I guess they have all moved on to the next location. All the more reason to stay.

My stomach growls as I make my way toward where I assume the kitchen is. It smells like tacos. It smells like heaven.

I stand just outside the door to the kitchen and listen to the men talking. I don't know how I'm supposed to go in there and eat with them like this is just a usual night for me. *How am I supposed to do that when every man in there has smuggled drugs and people? When they have killed or at least watched people being killed?*

I shake my head. *How am I any different?* I just watched a woman die. And I'm here. The only difference is, I'm not going to let them keep getting away with it.

I step into the kitchen, and the voices stop as everyone's eyes turn to me. My initial reaction is to smile politely at them, like I would if I were entering a boardroom. But I don't know how I'm supposed to react to a bunch of killers.

I smile politely at them and then walk over to the kitchen where there is a pot of meat and a tray of taco shells.

I grab a paper plate from the stack at the end and then place three shells on it. As I put meat in the shells, I feel everyone's eyes on me. I turn from the kitchen to the long table only a third filled with men.

I don't want to sit at that table. I want to take this food back to the room that is mine and eat in peace. That won't help me earn Nacio's or the men's trust though.

So, instead of going and hiding in my room upstairs, I march over to the table and sit in an open seat in the middle of the men. I ignore the surprised looks plastered on most of their faces. I honestly don't care, not when my stomach is growling loudly, signaling for me to eat the large plate of food I prepared myself.

I take a bite of the first taco, which practically melts in my mouth. It is a million times better than the slop they fed me when they were holding me in the room in the basement.

I scarf down the first taco as fast as I can, ignoring the roomful of men who are all looking at me. Usually, I would be too self-conscious to do anything, but today, I don't care. I scarf down the second taco before I look up at their stares.

The man sitting across from me is smiling brightly. "See? I told you all I could cook. If the girl likes it, then it must not be that bad."

"It still sucks balls," a man further down the table says. "I don't care if the girl likes it. It doesn't mean anything."

"Hey, first of all, the girl's name is Kinsley. And, second of all..." I look down at the plate of food and realize the meat is barely cooked. I have been consuming almost entirely raw beef. "And, second of all, this is terrible. I'm just starving, and I would eat anything right now."

The men all chuckle.

"See, Karp? I told you it was bad." The man sitting next to me grabs my plate with the one remaining taco on it. "Let me see if I can find you some real food."

I smile at him, thankful he is getting me more food that won't make me sick in the morning.

"Sorry, Kinsley," Karp says to me. "I was never taught to cook. I didn't think it would be that goddamn hard."

I smile. "It's okay. Just maybe leave the cooking to someone else in the future."

Karp smiles back. He looks young, at least a couple of years younger than me. His hair is dark and short. His body is short but fit. He doesn't look like a hard-core killer. He looks like a kid who has lost his way and doesn't know what to do.

"Here you go, *Kinsley*," the man says, emphasizing my name, as he places a new plate of food in front of me.

Tamales, I recognize immediately.

I dig in and realize this food is much better than what I was previously eating.

"Much better, right?"

I nod as I consume another mouthful.

The man smiles. "I'm Raul."

"Thanks Raul," I say through a mouthful.

Raul looks scary with tattoos covering his body and face, and he's almost double Karp's size.

"That's Samuel," he says, pointing to the man to my left. "You already met Seth." He smiles, pointing to the man who was my guard and held the gun up to my head earlier.

"Sorry about that," Seth says before taking a long drag of his beer.

I frown at him.

Raul continues, "The guy who cooked you the question-able food is Karp. And the quiet one over there is Ricardo. He doesn't speak much English."

I nod at Ricardo, who seems to be the oldest man in the room. I take another bite of my tamale and moan a little at how good it is until I see Raul looking at me with lust in his eyes. I force a smile and then return to eating without moaning.

"So, what do you guys typically do around here at this time of night?" I ask.

The men glance around to each other, not sure of what they are supposed to say or not say in front of me.

I stop eating. "Oh, come on, guys. I'm a Felton. You can tell me what you guys do."

The men continue to stare at one another, none of them wanting to speak.

Finally, Seth opens his mouth. "We are all on night shift tonight. None of us usually work nights, but since most of the men have moved to the other location, we have to cover more shifts. We are in charge of making sure no one gets in or *out* tonight."

I smile at him. "Good to know I'll have such strong men protecting me tonight." I take another bite. "So, where is the next location?"

Raul answers, "We don't know. They don't tell us shit."

I look around at all the men who are grumbling about not knowing where the next location is and that they should get to know something since they have all worked here long enough.

Seth looks at his phone. "We need to get going. Shift starts in five."

The men grumble some more but all begin to get up.

"Thanks again for the food," I say to Raul.

"Karp is also on cook duty tomorrow night. So, come to me, and I'll get you something edible."

"Thanks," I say.

I watch as the men all leave before I finish my plate of food. I get up from the rickety old table. I pick up the other empty plates the men left and throw them in the trash. I hate that these men made me feel anything for them at all. But they just seem like men. Not killers. Men who need a woman to pick up after them. Men who need a woman to teach them that what they are doing is wrong.

I yawn. I have no idea what time it is, other than knowing it is late based on how tired I feel. I should ask Nacio if they found my purse. That way, I can at least get my phone back.

I head upstairs through the old corridors until I find Nacio's office. I don't bother knocking. I just open the door and head in, just like Killian used to do to me.

His words, *"You find out the best information if you don't knock,"* ring in my ear. He's right.

As I enter Nacio's office, I hear Nacio use Killian's name, and I freeze. I glance around the room to see if Killian is here, but I see no one. *Please, God, don't let Killian really be involved with these people instead of the FBI. Please. Please just let him be an FBI agent.*

Nacio glances up at me with a frown on his face. He looks worn and worried for just a second at the sight of me, but then it disappears just as quickly. He ends his call without saying good-bye. Without any warning.

I walk over to the chair I pulled up to his desk as casually as possible, trying not to seem too interested in what he was saying. Trying not to seem bothered, but it is difficult. I take a seat in the hard chair and run my hand through my short locks.

His eyes focus intently on my hand as I do so. I let it slowly fall down my exposed neck. His eyes never leave my hand. His weakness is my sex appeal. That's the best way to get this man vulnerable enough so he trusts me. I just don't know if I can stomach flirting or doing more with this man.

"Who was that?"

He cocks his head to one side and shrugs. "I don't know what you are talking about."

I moisten my lips and watch as his eyes fall to my mouth. I take a guess. "Why were you talking to your brother about the FBI agent?"

Nacio's eyes darken, and he snaps out of the spell my body was drawing him under. "You'll find out soon enough."

I shake my head. "I'm not a very patient person. I want to know why, now."

"The FBI agent is in jail. His own people put him there. Just discussing if he is still a threat to us or not now that he is in jail."

I don't react to the news that Killian is in jail. In fact, I'm happy. It means he can't come after me. He can't try to save me. He's safe as long as he is there. After this is all over, the truth will come out. The truth that he is innocent.

"That's too bad. I would have liked to have seen him suffer more than that after what he did to me."

Nacio smiles at my harsh words. Words that are all a lie.

"Glad to hear you say that. I agree. The traitor deserves to suffer a lot more for what he has done."

I nod even though I don't know why Nacio hates Killian so much. He never did anything to Nacio. That's not true though, I realize. Killian knew this location, and my father trusted him enough to tell him some things.

Nacio stands from his chair and walks around his desk until he is leaning against it right in front of me. His legs are inches from my own. He reaches down and grabs my hand. He begins slowly massaging it.

I let him. He's just touching my hand, I reason. It's harmless although the look of lust on his face tells me he wants so much more. That he wants to fuck me. Or rape me. That he would take either one. That's not something that can happen. It's something I won't let happen.

"When are we going to the next location?" I ask, hoping to suck as much information as I can from him.

"In two days. We have a package arriving late tomorrow. We will leave the next night."

I nod. "How are we traveling?"

"Plane."

"Private or commercial?"

He shakes his head. "So many questions. No need to worry your pretty little head about issues like this. Everything is all taken care of. You don't need to worry about a thing. The plans have already been made."

I pull my hand out of his grasp. "I need to know if I'm going to help run things. I deserve to know."

"Not really. You don't deserve to know anything. Not yet. I already told you nobody becomes a part of this organization without paying their dues first. Even a Felton. Your father paid his dues. Your grandfather and his father before him. The same rules apply to you. Once you pass the tests, then you get to know. Not before then."

He crosses his arms and studies me now that he can no longer touch me like he wants to. Although, if he really wanted to, he could do whatever he wanted to me. He's stronger than me. He could overpower me in a second. That means, the only reason he isn't, is because I have something he needs. I just don't know what that is yet. *What power, other than his desire for me, do I hold? Is there something my father told me that Nacio wants to know?*

"You know, sweetheart, if you would just give in to me, I could make the rules disappear. You wouldn't have to pay your dues. You wouldn't have to wait for answers. I could tell you everything if you were mine. If you let me claim you. If you let me fuck you and marry you, then you wouldn't have to wait."

I raise my eyebrows at his absurd proposal. I stand up, and he straightens his body just a little until his body is pressed against mine.

"Really? You would do that for me? You would fuck me and marry me?"

Nacio grabs my ass, tightly pulling me against his

growing erection. "Yes, I would do that for you. It's what any princess like you would want. To be taken care of by a strong, competent man like me. I have money. I have power. You would never have to worry about a thing again."

"We would run the organization together, fifty-fifty?" I ask, letting him keep his hands on my ass, despite wanting to rip his arms off for what he is doing.

He shrugs. "Not fifty-fifty. The organization has never been run that way. There always has to be one person in power and one person who has less. But you wouldn't have to get your hands dirty. Admit it; this isn't the life for you. You don't want to kill people. That's not what you want. You just want the benefits that come from this business, just like you have always had. Marry me, and you would never have to worry about getting your hands dirty."

He grabs my neck. "And you would never have to worry about not being satisfied again," he whispers in my ear.

I try not to flinch as shivers travel throughout my body. But, this time, I'm not turned on by sexy words being whispered in my ear. My body shivers out of revulsion and tries to shake him off my body.

"Who's in control now? Who has the power now?"

"Me," he says.

I know he's lying. His eyes dilate, and his nostrils flare. He needs me to marry him and give him whatever power I have in this organization. It would give him the power he desperately seeks.

"What about your brother, my mother, my grandfather? If we married, what would we do with them? Wouldn't they be upset that they'll lose out on having the power in the organization?"

He smiles and then licks his lips, like a tiger would just

before it pounced on its meal. He thinks he's won, and I'm the meal.

"I wouldn't worry about them. They couldn't protest if we were already married."

I glance over his shoulder, unable to look at his lust-filled eyes any longer. I have to keep a look of disgust off my face. I look at his desk, trying to decide on what I'm going to do. *Do I say yes? Would that be easier? Or do I say hell no and try to find another way to gain his trust?*

That's when I see it. My purse is sitting on the corner of his desk. He's known who I am the whole time. The whole time he had me locked in the basement, he knew who I was, and he still kept me locked up like I was a dog. He thinks he can control me and do whatever the fuck he wants with me.

He's wrong.

I glance back to Nacio, who has a smug look on his face.

"So, what do you say, sweetheart?"

Nacio leans down to my neck to kiss me, but I don't let him get that far. I take my knee and knee him in the groin as hard as I can.

He releases me and grabs his groin as he writhes in pain. I walk around to the other side of his desk and grab my purse.

"I told you I would remove your balls if you touched me again without my permission. Don't do it again."

He looks at me with a deep grimace. His eyes have turned darker, and I know I shouldn't have done that. He will make me pay for hurting him. I don't think anybody gets away with hurting him without paying. But it was worth it. Whatever he does to me, I can take it just to see the look of shock and pain on his disgusting face.

I hold up my purse to him. He doesn't say anything. He just keeps grabbing his balls.

"You knew who I was the whole time. You had my purse, and I'm sure you went through it. You knew, and you still kept me locked up." I glance down at his crotch. "Call us even now."

I check that my phone, ID, and money are still in my purse before I walk around the desk and head toward the door. I pause and turn back to Nacio when I reach the door.

"I'm going to sleep now. Alone. And, if anybody enters my room tonight, I will do much worse than just kick them in the balls. Tomorrow, I will need a car to go into town to get some new clothes. I can't keep wearing this forever."

I turn back, thinking I've won. I grab the door and begin to open it when the door suddenly gets slammed shut in my face.

"No. You will not get a car to go into town. You will not leave without permission. Like I said before, you have not passed my tests yet. You don't leave the premises until then. I will have someone go into town and get some clothes that are more revealing than the granny clothes you have on now."

He glances up and down my body, but I know he is lying and just trying to get under my skin. My halter top and pants are plenty revealing enough.

"And, if you think about leaving, I will know. There are video cameras in every hallway. You can't leave without me knowing. Tomorrow, you will have your second test, so get some sleep, sweetheart. If you don't pass, you won't get out of here alive."

I narrow my eyes at him. I hate him. I hate the tone of his voice as he threatens my life. It's so casual, yet I can tell it excites him, thinking about killing me. I realize I might have chosen wrong. I don't know what the next test is. I don't know if I can do it. If one of the tests involves killing someone innocent, I don't think I'll be able to do it. It might have been easier to marry him and sleep with him. And, if that is the case, I might as well take his gun and pull the trigger myself because I can't let that happen.

Instead, I grab the doorknob again, and I leave without another word to Nacio. He doesn't get to see my fear. He doesn't get to know I'm already dead.

I walk back to the room that Nacio told me was mine. I open the door and step inside the smelly, dark room. I don't bother turning on the lights when I enter. I prefer the darkness right now. I close the door behind me, and I lock it, but I know the flimsy lock will be useless. If any of the men decide they want to come in, they can do so without putting a drop of effort into it.

I walk through the room, passing bunk bed after bunk bed. I only stop when I bump my leg against the corner of one of the bunks in the far corner of the room. I look at the sheets on the bottom bunk that I know have never been washed. This is as good as it is going to get right now.

Unless I say yes to Nacio. Then, I could sleep where he sleeps. I could sleep in a nice, plush bed I'm sure is fit for a king instead of this dank, dark room.

I try not to think about Nacio as I lie down on the bed. I don't bother to crawl under the covers. I just lie right on top. I don't take my clothes or shoes off either. I can't stand to take my clothes off—not in a place like this, with men like this. I need to be able to make a quick escape even though I know a quick escape doesn't exist, not unless the escape is at the end of a gun.

Tears begin falling in cascades now. Tears that should have fallen long ago now make their way down my face until my eyes are burning from the smeared mascara and eye shadow stinging my eyes from not washing it off in days. I need to shower. I need clean clothes. I need makeup.

But my needs seem silly compared to what I just witnessed today. I saw a girl die because of me. She died simply because she looked like me. That's a terrible reason to die. And that's a terrible reason to watch someone die.

I close my eyes, trying to push the woman out of my head, but her blue eyes and blonde hair keep coming back to haunt me. There is nothing I can do about it. I will never be able to sleep again.

9

———

KILLIAN

I OPEN MY EYES. I don't see anything but darkness. My head hurts like a motherfucker. I try to rub my head to ease some of the pain, but my arms are met with resistance. Rope is wrapped tightly against my arms, keeping them tied behind my back. I try to slip my hands out of the rope, but it is no use. Whoever tied my hands behind my back has done this a time or two. They knew what the fuck they were doing. I won't be able to break free. Houdini couldn't break out of these ropes.

My shoulders begin hurting from being in an awkward position, and I feel the ropes burning into my wrists. I don't care though. The pain actually makes me feel better. It reminds me of my mission. It reminds me that I have to seek my revenge for Kinsley. I just have to figure out how to get out of here first.

The box truck bounces as we go over a bump. My head bounces hard against the truck wall.

"Fuck," I moan as the pounding in my head gets worse.

I try to figure out my surroundings in the back of the truck, but it is hard in the darkness. It's not the same truck

Santino and I rode in when we broke out of jail. This truck is much smaller than that one, and as far as I can tell, I am the only one or thing back here.

My legs aren't tied, just my hands, so I adjust them to push against the wall until I'm in a standing position. I walk slowly to the back door of the truck, trying not to fall, despite the truck bouncing at every curve. If I could get the door open, then I could jump and make a run for it. It would be risky, but what other option do I have? My only other option is to stay in the truck and wait for them to kill me. Even if they don't kill me, whatever they have planned for me can't be good. I know that much. And I'm not going to just sit on my ass and wait to find out.

I just wish I knew where I am. Somewhere rural? Urban? The middle of nowhere?

If I'm going to make a break for it, I would much rather do it somewhere urban where I can get to a phone. To people. If I break out in the middle of nowhere, I don't stand a chance. They could take their time in tracking me down with guns. They could run me over with the truck. I'd be fucked.

I can't focus on that though. There are no windows, so I have no idea where we are. All I need to focus on is getting this fucking door open and then running as fast as I can. And, if I die, so be it.

I put my foot down where the latch is and pull hard until it turns over. I'm a little shocked that it actually worked. I thought for sure they would have put a lock on the outside of the door. These guys aren't as experienced as I first thought.

I regain my balance as we round another corner, and then I put my foot back under the latch. My heart is beating fast. This is it. As soon as I lift it, the door will make a loud noise, alerting the driver that it is open. So, no matter what I see on the other side, I have to be ready to run as soon as I open the door.

The truck slows a little, and I know this is my chance. I lift my foot hard and fast, trying to give as much momentum to get the door moving upright. It moves about halfway open. It's enough for me to jump out.

Buildings. I see large buildings. *Thank God. I have a chance.*

I don't have time to decide which building is my best bet to run toward. I don't have time to make a plan. I jump from the truck, somehow landing my feet on what I realize is a rocky dirt road instead of the pavement it should be in such an urban area. I don't have time to think about it though. I just run.

I run straight ahead for a block and then duck down an alleyway. I don't hear the truck turn around behind me. I don't hear footsteps either, but that doesn't mean someone isn't there. I keep running down the alleyway, trying to get as far away as possible, before I decide to duck in somewhere to get help.

But, as I run, I begin to lose hope I'm going to find anyone who can help me. As I run, I realize where I am— the one place I never wanted to return to, yet knew I would have to one day.

Yet this is the one place I wanted to be. This is where I'll get revenge for Kinsley. This is where I'll make things right. But I won't find help here because there is no one here who can help. There's only darkness and hatred. Only danger.

I keep running though, hoping I can find someplace to hide until I can get these ropes off and find a weapon to kill them.

But I don't get the chance.

I turn the corner, and Santino is standing with a gun pointed at me. I freeze. I consider turning and running in the opposite direction, but I was wrong. These guys are experts. They do this for a living. If he pulls that trigger, he won't miss, so I don't move. This isn't my chance. I will have to try again—if I get another opportunity.

Santino walks slowly toward me, the gun pointing straight at my head. I don't focus on the gun. I don't know if it's my training or what that tells me to keep my eyes on the shooter and not the gun. The gun isn't what is going to kill me; the shooter will. The shooter's eyes will tell me if he is going to shoot or not. By the time his finger pulls the trigger, it is too late to react.

And Santino's eyes are telling me he doesn't want to shoot me, but he will if I run. I don't understand what he needs me for, but I'll be patient long enough to find out. So, I stay in place as Santino moves closer and closer.

He grabs ahold of my shoulder to turn me around as he presses the barrel of the gun to my head. "Walk," he says.

I walk. When we make it out of the alleyway, another man comes over and holds on to my other arm, but Santino doesn't remove the gun from my head.

The buildings become more and more familiar as we walk through the city until the one I recognize comes into view. The door is still barely hanging on to the hinges. We don't pause at the door though. Santino doesn't knock. He just pushes me inside where I know I will never return. There are only two reasons they would bring me here—to get some info out of me and to kill me. There is no other reason.

I just have to find a way to kill as many of these mother-fuckers as I can before I go. That way, Kinsley's death won't be for nothing.

Santino walks next to me, the gun still firm against my head, as the other man trails off behind me. I can't tell, but he most likely has a gun on me as well.

We walk down a hallway, and I hear voices. One voice in particular sounds familiar. It's the same voice I heard that night when I came here. The same voice I heard at the casino. It's almost identical to Santino's voice. It's a wonder I didn't recognize Santino's voice before.

We round a corner, and the voices get louder.

"In here." Santino grabs my arms and jerks me into a large room full of people.

The contrast between the dark hallway and the light room blinds me at first. I close my eyes and then open them again, trying to get them to adjust quickly.

"Good job, brother. I wasn't sure if I could count on you to do this job, but you've proven your worth," a man says in a similar voice to Santino.

I see the man stand up from the table of men who have now grown silent. The man walks over to us, and I see he is definitely Santino's brother. He has the same coloring and facial structure, although this man is a little taller and slightly older than Santino. And his hair is long, compared with Santino's buzzed head. But I realize now they both have the same eyes. Eyes that are out for blood.

"I'm Nacio," the man says. "Glad you could finally join us."

I glare at him but don't say anything. I don't know what his role is here yet. I won't disrespect him and get myself killed until I have killed the person responsible for Kinsley's death.

The man turns to the far side of the room. "Sweetheart, will you come here?"

He motions to the side of the room. My stomach churns

as I think about whatever vile woman would think so little of other women to be with a man who treats women like property, like dirt. I can't imagine such a woman.

A woman stands at the far side of the table. She doesn't look at me. All I can see are her dark pants and black lacy bra. She doesn't even bother to wear a shirt. My eyes travel up though and then stop at the chopped off blonde locks.

It can't be...

The woman turns to me, and I see...

"Kinsley?" the word falls from my lips as she walks to Nacio's side.

She barely looks at me though and then turns her attention to Nacio.

She's alive. My heart beats wildly as I see her here, alive. I don't know how it's possible, and I don't really care. All I know is, my heart has a reason to keep beating. My lungs have a reason to keep breathing.

Somehow, the universe has answered prayers I never asked because I thought it was impossible.

She's alive. Kinsley is standing no more than five feet away from me, and I want nothing more than to run to her, tackle her to the ground, and kiss her like crazy.

I feel a tear welling up in my eyes. A tear of pure joy. It drops quickly down my cheek, so fast I'm not even sure if anyone notices.

"You know how you told me you wanted to kill the FBI agent who destroyed your life?" Nacio says to Kinsley. "Well, I had my brother get him for you. I agree he deserves a lot worse than just going to jail. I want him to really pay for what he did, too, so I brought him here for you."

Kinsley doesn't look at me as he's talking. Instead, she looks at him. A slow grin forms on her face at his words. A smile I have never seen before. A smile I don't understand.

"What do you think about that, sweetheart?"

Every time he calls her that, I want to hurt him. I want to bring him as much pain as he brings me when he calls my girl that. I can't stand it.

"Thank you," Kinsley says simply, a smile still on her face.

"Really? I break him out of jail for you, and that's all the thanks I get? If I had known you didn't really mean what you said last night, I wouldn't have bothered."

When he finishes speaking, she doesn't hesitate. She walks straight to him, grabs his neck, and solidly kisses him on the lips.

I lose it. I move toward them, intending to put a stop to it, when Santino grabs my arm.

"You move, and I'll kill you," he says.

I stop moving. But I can't fucking look at her kissing another man. I close my eyes and wait until she finishes the kiss.

I can't believe her. I can't believe she would willingly kiss another man. I thought I was her life. I was wrong. I'm a fucking idiot.

I should have chosen the FBI, not her. She's willingly working here. She could have left at anytime, but instead, she's staying here. For all I know, she's been participating in the smuggling, in the rapes, in the killings. She is a monster, just like everyone else in this room.

"Thank you," she says.

I open my eyes to a smug Nacio beaming from the kiss, like he just won.

He won.

I lost.

Now, I just want them to get this over with and put a bullet between my eyes.

"It doesn't change anything, Nacio. I'm not going to marry you," Kinsley says.

Nacio's face drops a little.

The men around the room are all staring at the exchange between the two of them. I suspect that was not something Nacio wanted Kinsley to share with everyone. He didn't want her to share that she had turned down his proposal, but it makes me feel better to know she isn't going to marry the smug fucker—at least, not yet.

He raises his eyebrows at Kinsley, but she stands defiantly next to him, not backing down. I don't quite understand the relationship between the two, but if I know anything about Kinsley—which I'm not sure I do—I know she is stubborn as hell and won't back down, not when she decides on what she really wants.

Nacio walks over to her and whispers something in her ear. She frowns but doesn't say anything further.

Nacio pulls a gun out of the back of his jeans and hands it to Kinsley. "Kill him," Nacio says to her while motioning to me.

"What?" she says, frozen with the gun in her hand.

Kill him, I think. *Kill Nacio.*

We won't survive, but at least the ringleader in all of this would be dead, too. At least the man who forced Kinsley to kiss him would be dead.

"Kill the FBI agent. After all, he's the reason your father is dead. Kill him, and avenge your father."

10

KINSLEY

I HOLD the gun in my hand. It's heavier than I thought it would be. For such a small thing, it feels bulky in my hand. I can't stop staring at it.

This tiny object is the cause of so many people dying. So many lives have been lost all because of this weapon. Those lives might not have been lost if the person hadn't had a weapon that so easily separated them from the crime they were committing. If they'd had to use a knife instead of a gun, would so many killings have happened? If they'd had to get their hands dirty with the victim's blood, would they still have done it? If they'd had to really think about it and plan it with a bomb, would they still have done it?

I hold the gun in my hand. How easy it would be for me to aim the gun at Killian and pull the trigger. It wouldn't even feel like I'm really killing him because this gun doesn't feel dangerous. It doesn't feel any different than holding any other inanimate object. But it is. This object is the most powerful of all.

I could do it. I could kill Killian and secure my place here. I would have all the power if I did. I know Nacio thinks I can't do it. He's still suspicious of why I'm here. He thinks I still love Killian.

He's right. I do.

The second I saw Killian walk into the cafeteria, my heart stopped. The one thing I was trying to prevent from happening has happened. And, now, everything I have been through over the last few days without Killian has been for nothing. Now, we are both going to die.

I tried to hide behind the table of men blocking Killian from me. I thought if I hid, nobody would be able to see my feelings so clearly plastered all over my face. There's no way for me to hide how I feel about Killian.

When Nacio called me to the center of the room, I couldn't bear to look at Killian for more than one second. If I did that, the whole room would know I still love Killian, I always did. They would know and shoot us both without a second thought. So, I tried to remain frozen. I tried to remain careless. I tried to look at anybody but Killian, tied, standing in front of me.

When I saw him so broken and in so much pain at the sight of me, I almost couldn't stand it myself. I couldn't stand remaining by Nacio and not running to Killian. Even if it meant we would both die, it meant I could die wrapped in his arms. I could die loving him. Death might be worth one final embrace. One final kiss.

I didn't though. I stayed by Nacio's side. And I did the only thing I could think of that would make Nacio less suspicious about my relationship with Killian. I kissed Nacio.

It wasn't a gentle, chaste kiss either. I forced my tongue into Nacio's mouth as our lips collided together. I grabbed the nape of this neck, keeping his lips firmly against mine. I moaned just a little as his tongue pressed against mine. I put everything I could into the kiss.

And, now, I won't be able to live with myself for doing it. I won't be able to live with myself for kissing anyone but Killian. I won't be able to forgive myself for kissing another man in front of Killian, especially since that might be the last image of me he ever sees. I hate that I put a small drop of doubt into Killian's head, making him think I don't love him. But I already did that with the note I wrote him. I already planted that seed in his head. With the kiss, I just confirmed he means nothing to me.

I shiver from the cold draft in the room, bringing me back to the present. I resist the urge to wrap my arm around my chest to warm myself. I hate that I'm basically wearing a bra in front of a dozen men, but I can't let Nacio see me as weak. He has to see me as an equal, so I won't let him know he has won with the clothing he bought for me, considering this outfit was the most covered one he bought. I should be thankful for the clothing. Revealing clothing makes it easier to control these men. It makes it easier for them to think I am only a sex object and not a person who schemes and plans and wants power of her own.

"On your knees," Santino says to Killian.

I glance up in time to see that Killian hasn't moved. He's standing tall in front of us, just like he always does. Santino forces him into a kneeling position. I don't know why it matters whether he stands or kneels if he is going to be shot and killed either way. I guess kneeling makes it easier for me to shoot him. If he's standing, he might run at the last second.

I take a chance and look into Killian's eyes as he kneels in front of me. They're dark and intense, like always. When I look at them, I realize he's in a lot of pain, not necessarily physical but just pain. I've hurt him in unforgivable ways, but I still see love there. When I see it, I look away, back to the gun in my hand, hoping I am the only one who can see the love still there in his eyes.

"Kill him," Nacio commands again from behind me.

What I really want to do is kill Nacio. He deserves it for what he's done. If I did that though, all the men sitting at the table on either side would shoot me next before I even had a chance to react.

"Kill him for what he did to your father," Nacio says.

I have to know. Before I figure out if I have any options other than killing Killian, I have to know what Nacio is talking about.

"What do you mean, Killian killed my father?" I ask Nacio.

"Killian is the reason your father is dead. Your father didn't die from a heart attack. Killian killed him."

"Why? Why would he do that?"

"When your father found out Killian was FBI, Killian did the only thing he could to save himself. He killed your father first before your father could kill him, before his cover was blown and we found out he was FBI."

Nacio smirks at Killian. "We found out anyway."

"Lies!" Killian screams suddenly from the ground. "It's all lies!"

I glance from Nacio to Killian in time to see Killian getting kicked in the back by Santino.

"Shut up, or I'll shoot you myself," Santino says.

Killian squeezes his eyes shut, most likely dealing with the pain from being kicked hard in the back. I watch his breathing become uneven as he tries to deal with the pain.

I turn back to Nacio, unable to watch Killian in agony without feeling it myself. But, when Nacio speaks about

Killian killing my father, he doesn't seem to be lying. He's telling the truth—or what he believes to be true. Killian was involved in my father's death. I just don't know in what way exactly.

A week or two ago, that would have hurt me to find out Killian might have been the one who killed my father. Now though, it barely stings since I know my father got what he deserved. He probably deserved even worse.

I turn back to Killian. He lied though. Again, he lied. And I have to make it known I'm not happy about it.

I walk toward him, my eyes focused on his. I can't show him anything but the anger I let surface from another lie he told me. Another lie that hurts me. That's all I get—lie after lie after lie from him. Never the truth. With him, there is always something more hidden.

I walk until I'm standing right in front of him. I'm fuming. I feel everyone's eyes on me, all unsure of what I'm going to do. Kill him? Question him? Forgive him?

I try to feel the anger as best as I can as I look Killian in the eyes. All I see is love and truth. Truth I never expected to see. He thinks I've moved forward to kill him. He thinks these are his final seconds alive, and with those seconds, he is going to love me.

I hate that he thinks that. I hate that I could kill him, and he would still love me with his last breath.

I bend down, so I can look eye-to-eye with Killian for what he thinks is going to be the last time. I glare at him with my blue eyes while his soften with more love. He's trying his best to tell me it's okay, he understands why I'm doing this.

I stand back up. "This is for killing my father," I say. I raise the gun and hit it against Killian's head as hard as I can.

I hear a gasp from someone behind me. I watch as Killian's head whips to the side, and I am surprised to see a gush of blood spill from his lips where I hit him instead of the side of his head where I aimed.

I glance up and see Santino smiling smugly behind Killian, happy I'm on their side instead of Killian's.

I watch Killian put his head back upright, and I'm scared at how much blood covers his face. I can't hit him in the head again, like I was planning. It would cause too much damage. Too much pain.

He opens his eyes, even though one is bloody, despite the torment I know he must be feeling.

I kick him hard in the stomach with the heel of my shoe. I watch as he falls backward. He hits his head again on the hard concrete floor.

I take a step forward so I'm standing over him. "That was for me. For lying to me about who you were and pretending to love me when all you were really doing was framing my family to meet your own needs."

I spit on him in disgust and then turn away, hoping I didn't give him a concussion or cause any other permanent damage.

"Kneel, you motherfucker," Santino says.

Killian moans as he is forced back into a kneeling position.

I try to ignore the pain I hear coming from him. Instead, I focus on the wicked gleam in Nacio's eyes. He's impressed by what I've done. If I shot Killian now, he would believe I was on his side. Even if I didn't kill Killian, one shot would be enough.

I can't though. I can't shoot him, and I can't let anyone else either. So, I think of the one thing that might give

Killian one more day to live even if it means I'm risking my own life to do it.

I lift the gun and place it in Nacio's hands. "We can't kill him," I say.

Nacio frowns at me in disappointment. "Don't you mean, *you* can't kill him? I'm disappointed in you, sweetheart. After the performance you just gave, I thought putting a bullet between his eyes would be the easy part."

Nacio takes the gun and begins walking toward Killian with the same intensity he had when he walked me to the room with the blonde girl he killed. I grab his arm and turn him back to me.

"You can't kill him either. We still need him, baby," I say, adding the term of endearment to the end, despite how much it kills me to.

"And why not?"

I stroke his cheek, buying myself more time to figure out a reason.

I smile when I finally have an answer. "Because the FBI might already know where our next base of operation is. They could follow us or get here before we leave. He's our only insurance. We need to figure out what he knows and then keep him alive until we are sure the FBI is no longer invested in going after us. Then, we will get rid of him. The FBI will simply think we turned him. They saw him leaving the jail of his own accord with Santino, after all."

Nacio smiles and then tangles his hand in my hair before pulling me into a wet, hungry kiss. He releases me a few seconds later. "Beauty and brains. Who knew?" Then, he says, "Seth."

Seth stands from the table.

"Take him upstairs and see what he knows. After you

find out what he knows, keep him upstairs and get him ready to be transferred tomorrow. Understood?"

"Yes, sir," Seth says.

Seth signals for two other men to follow him and then goes over to Killian. I watch as they force him back into a standing position. Killian doesn't take his eyes off of me though. Not until he is forced to turn away from me and walk out the door.

I don't know what kind of pain I've just subjected Killian to. I don't know what torture they will use to get him to talk. I just hope he talks. He needs to survive long enough for me to find a way for him to get out of here.

I don't know how much time that is. One night? Two? I don't know how much time I have left to keep him alive. But that is my new mission. Keep Killian alive, and then I can worry about the rest.

When Killian is no longer in view, Santino walks over to where Nacio and I are still standing.

"So, you're the infamous Kinsley Felton," Santino says to me.

"Yes. And you're Nacio's younger brother, Santino."

Santino smiles brightly, showing off his sparkly white teeth. "So, my brother did talk about me while I was gone. I wish he had talked to me about you. I would have gotten here faster if I'd known how beautiful you were. You think you can kiss me like you did my brother? After all, I deserve a kiss, too, for breaking Killian out of jail for you."

I don't have to answer though because Nacio throws a punch in Santino's direction. Santino ducks, expecting the punch. He laughs as Nacio's face reddens and darkens at the thought of Santino kissing me.

"Chill, dude. I was just joking. You know I would never mess with a girl you already claimed. Not when a dozen more just like her that I could fuck with less trouble are upstairs right now. I'm just messing with you. Lighten up, man."

Nacio's face lightens, but his eyes stay dark and angry. "I'm heading into town for a couple of hours to pick up some things. Want to come, baby?" he asks me.

Santino interjects, "Or you could stay with me, and I could show you around. I know my boring brother didn't do that great of a job." He smiles at me, expecting me to take Nacio up on his offer.

But I don't want to leave the premises, not now that Killian is here. I can't take a chance that whoever remains behind will change their mind and just kill him. I also don't know why Nacio will let me leave the premises with him when, earlier today, he was so stern about me not being able to leave.

"I'll stay with Santino," I say to Nacio. "I need to get to know both of the people I will be working with."

Santino slings his arm around my shoulders in a way I wasn't expecting. "Don't worry, brother. I won't do anything you wouldn't do."

I smile. I can't help it. Santino's smile is infectious.

Nacio glares at the pair of us. "Fine. I didn't show her how the men get paid. You can start with that."

"Boring," Santino says flatly.

"Do it. I'll be back in an hour, and then we can discuss transportation plans for tomorrow."

Santino rolls his eyes but nods at his brother.

Nacio walks to me, stopping too close for my comfort. "This doesn't mean you have passed yet. When we arrive at our next location you will still have to kill him to pass the test. Until then, the same rules apply."

I nod. "I didn't think they wouldn't apply."

"Good." Nacio says to his brother, "Behave," before he walks out of the room, leaving me along with Santino.

Santino pulls his leather jacket off and hands it to me. "Here. You look cold."

I notice the goose bumps covering my arms and torso. "Thanks."

"My brother can be a bit of a jackass. Don't let your opinion of him influence your opinion of me though. I'm much nicer and a lot more fun than he is."

I smile as I slip into his jacket, thankful to be more covered up.

He holds out his arm, and I take it, like he's my prom date.

"Come on, I can show you the boring paperwork to appease my brother, and then we can find something more fun to get into before he gets back."

I nod, and he guides me out of the cafeteria and up the stairs to the offices. He leads me into an office next to Nacio's. This one is slightly smaller than Nacio's, but otherwise, it looks exactly the same.

"Pull up a chair next to my desk," Santino says as he takes a seat behind his desk.

From his desk, he begins pulling out envelopes with names written on them. He starts typing on his computer, and I pull up a chair next to him behind his desk, so I can see what he is doing.

He has a spreadsheet with names pulled up. But they aren't regular names. They are code names, I realize. Even if someone took this computer, no one would have any legal names or any way to track the business. That basically means, if I or the FBI took it, the computer would be useless.

"These are all code names we use for the guys who work

for us. We also use this system to tag all the people, drugs, and money, but we will explain that part of the system later when we get..."

I suck in a breath, waiting for him to tell me where, but he catches himself.

"Anyway, only the people at the top know how to read the code names. It is a boring, tricky process to assign men code names and remember them since we don't have any sort of key written down anywhere. You just have to remember. Once you start meeting all the guys, we will help you memorize them."

"Do the men know their own code names?"

"No. We call them by whatever first name they tell us. I don't even think the names they tell us are their real names, and it honestly doesn't matter to us. We find out their real names anyway and then do extensive background checks on all our men regardless of what they want to be called. This is just a system to keep their real names off the books."

I nod.

"Anyway, you don't need to worry about any of this right now. All you need to worry about is the hierarchy of the men and how they get paid."

I nod again.

"Our men get paid every six months."

I raise my eyebrows. "Why so long? Don't the men get upset with having to wait that long to get paid? How do they pay their bills?"

"No, they don't get upset. They know up front how long it will be until they get paid. And all of their living costs are paid for as long as they work for us."

"What about their families?"

"Their families are taken care of—if they survive six months. If they survive, we will pay for basic expenses for their families as well. And the money they make is more than most of these men would make in a lifetime. We are very generous employers."

"But why make them wait six months until they get paid?"

He smiles. "Loyalty. We want loyal employees who will stay with us forever. Doing what we do, we need people who will be devoted to us for life. We don't want people who are only in this for a quick paycheck. That's why we reward loyalty, not position. The longer you are with us, the more you get paid."

"There aren't higher and lower positions?"

"There is us and them. There are the Marlows and Feltons, and then there is everybody else. Everybody else does whatever position we ask them to do. Sure, there are people we trust more than others, but everybody gets the same, depending on how long they have been with us. Tomorrow, we could have different needs. For example, our most trusted person who is responsible for shipping might have to be responsible for night-shift guard duty the next night. We reward loyalty above everything else."

"But what motivation do the men have for doing a good job if they aren't going to get paid accordingly?"

He cocks his head to the side in the same way that Nacio does, except Santino has a small dimple on his cheek. I notice it when he smiles, making him seem less harmful than Nacio.

But, as he leans forward and pulls his gun out from his jeans, I know he is equally as dangerous, despite the dimple.

"This," he says, holding his gun. "This is why the men listen and do what they are told without question. They know they will be eliminated if they don't. We don't give second chances."

I nod slowly as he puts the gun back in the back of his jeans.

Santino turns his attention back to the screen. "So, as you can see, we mark off six-month periods, and for every period they last, they get a five percent increase."

"How long do the men typically last?"

He shrugs. "If they make it six months with us, they usually last a lifetime. But less than twenty percent make it to six months."

I gulp, not wanting to know the answer to my next question, but I ask anyway, "Do you kill them if they don't make it to six months?"

He actually laughs at my question, like it is the most bizarre thing I could have ever asked.

I stare blankly at him. I have no idea what I said that was so funny.

He stops laughing suddenly when he sees my face. "Sorry, but I thought the answer to that would have been obvious. Yes. If they don't make it to six months, then they have to go. Once you start working for us, it is a lifetime commitment. We can't chance them telling someone about what we do."

I want to ask for exact details. I know they smuggle, but from where to where? Why? How? I want to ask all the questions, but I don't.

"We have two men coming up on six months, so it's time to pay them."

"Why do most of the men that make it to six months last?"

"By then, they have seen the worst. They have killed

people. They have gotten their hands dirty. And because of this..." He points to the screen.

When I see the large number, my mouth drops open. I stare in disbelief at what these men make in six months if they last that long. It's half a million. They make half a million US dollars if they can last six months.

"Once they get that first large paycheck, they are hooked."

I nod, understanding now. "How do we pay them?"

"Cash."

"How do we give them that much cash at one time?"

"We don't. At the six-month mark, we give them the cash in a few increments over the next month or two. When you see an envelope full of cash, it does something to you. The men will suddenly do anything for you. Things they wouldn't do before, they do now."

"But why wouldn't they just quit after that first paycheck?"

"First of all, nobody quits, remember? And, second of all, they get hooked. They get used to that money and want more and more of it. They can't stop."

I still don't understand fully, but I guess it makes sense because our families have been getting away with this for years without getting caught, so whatever they are doing must be working.

I hear a knock on the door, and we both look up.

Santino exits the program on the computer. "Come in," he says.

The door opens, and Seth walks in.

"I have the info the FBI agent told us."

"Good. Proceed," Santino says.

Seth looks to me and then back to Santino, unsure if he should be speaking.

"It's okay, Seth. Kinsley is one of us now. If she messes up, she'll be dead. Anything you have to say, you can say in front of her."

Seth hesitates for another second, shifting his weight from side to side, before he finally speaks, "He says the FBI found the bodies. They are investigating what happened and believe they can figure out the location based on the evidence at the scene. They are assembling a team to move in."

"Excellent. Anything else, Seth?"

Seth looks down at his feet and then to me. "He's still in love with her," he says, looking at me.

Santino raises his eyebrows. "Anything else?"

"No, sir."

"Good."

Seth turns to leave, passing Raul who stands hesitantly in the doorway as Seth passes him.

"Come in." Santino sighs, like this is how he spends most of his day and he hates it.

I hate that Seth said Killian still loves me. It means that at least one person was observant because I know Killian would never admit to that and put me at risk on his own. It makes it even more important for him to get out of here.

Raul comes in next. He's out of breath and panting hard. He holds his chest, trying to slow his breathing so he can speak. It takes him several seconds, but he is finally able to get the words out. "Security system...it's down."

"Shit," Santino says, quickly getting up from his chair.

I watch as the chair falls over, and then I quickly get up, too. I run after Santino as he walks out of the office. I'm not going to miss a chance to check out how the security is set up.

I follow Santino down the stairs, past the cafeteria, and into a small dark room.

"I don't know what happened," Karp says, pointing to the screens. "I didn't do anything."

"Out of the way," Santino snarls at Karp, pushing him out of the way.

Santino sits down at the computers that are black instead of surveilling the building. Santino begins pushing buttons and turning things off and on, trying to get the screens to work again. But it doesn't work.

"Go get Seth," Santino says to Karp. "And, Karp, you'd better hope we can get this back up and running."

Santino's threat is obvious. Karp's job and life depend on getting the security systems back up and running.

I stand, watching Santino try thing after thing, but nothing happens. I glance to the cord behind Santino and see the easy solution to the problem. I shouldn't tell him. It is to my advantage if the security systems stay down. But I can't let Karp die for a simple mistake. Maybe it will earn me some points to fix the security system.

I bend down and plug the cord back into the wall. I watch as the screens roar to life. I watch as Santino's lips curl back into a smile of relief. I doubt Nacio would be happy to return to find the security systems down. Santino stares at me.

"The outlet is flimsy. If we were staying here, I would recommend it be replaced. You should let whoever is on security duty next know the cord could fall out of the outlet again."

Santino just stares at me until Seth comes into the small room.

"Sir?"

Santino stops staring. "The security system was down,

but I got it up and running again. It seems the cord fell out of the outlet. You are on duty tonight, so I just wanted you to know how to fix it if it happened again."

Seth nods.

Santino turns back to the screens and begins checking that everything is in place. I look over his shoulder, trying my best to see where the cameras are located.

I take a deep breath when a screen switches to the hallway. The hallway that will forever haunt my dreams. I wait for the cameras to switch to one of the rooms. I wait to come face-to-face with the room where I watched the woman die. I wait for the cameras to show me Killian tied up in a room somewhere. I wait for the cameras to show me all of the other broken people who are trapped in the rooms upstairs. I wait, but the cameras never go into any of the rooms. Instead, they just skim the hallways and exits.

There are no cameras in any of the rooms.

The thought sounds over and over again in my head.

There are no cameras in any of the rooms.

That means, I can visit Killian. My heart beats rapidly in my chest at the thought of having a few seconds alone with him. I could do it. I could go to his room. I just need to find out which room he is in, and I need an excuse for being in his room. But that is all details. Because I can go see Killian. And that is all that matters.

11

KILLIAN

I DEEPLY BREATHE OUT, trying to rid my body of the pain that has inched its way into every corner of my body. My arms are sore from being tied up on either side of my head, making my muscles ache.

I can barely think straight due to the pounding, stabbing pain continuously nagging my head. Blood still drips from my lips and eye where Kinsley hit me. My back stings from being whipped multiple times, and my stomach is bruised from Kinsley's kick.

Overall though, the physical pain is nothing compared to the emotional pain I'm dealing with. I'm lucky really. The pain I endured after I was brought to this room was nothing. The simple whipping stopped as soon as I started talking. It wasn't real torture. The men who were whipping me, their hearts weren't in it. They were just doing their job.

Real torture only happens when people truly care about what they are doing. When they aren't trying to get information out of someone but instead doing it because they enjoy the torture themselves. That's not what I experienced.

If I'm lucky enough to live another night, I have a feeling

I will get to experience real torture at the hands of Nacio or Santino. They hate me. They have a reason to torture me. They have a reason to make me pay for the trouble I've put them through.

But the discomfort they have dealt with is nothing compared to what they have put me through these last few days. The misery from thinking Kinsley was dead was unbearable. I shouldn't have survived it. Somehow though, I'm still alive, barely hanging on. Somehow, I've managed to live long enough to see Kinsley alive again.

It's enough, seeing her alive. It's enough to make all the pain I went through worth it. It's enough to make my death worth it. My death that I know will be coming soon.

Kinsley barely kept me alive today. She found a way to keep me alive, but I don't know if she is keeping me alive for my benefit or hers. I don't even know if she still loves me or just wasn't heartless enough to kill me—yet.

But, either way, the only way she will survive more than a couple of days is to kill me. And dying to keep the woman I love alive is more than worth it. I would give my life a hundred times if it meant she would get to live. It's all I care about anymore. All I care about is that she lives.

That is my only mission—to keep her alive at all costs.

I don't care why she is here. To join them. To bring them down. To protect her family. I don't care. She must survive this.

My eyes grow heavy with each second, so heavy that I must sleep, but sleep won't come easily. Not when my hands are tied up above my head and I'm stuck sitting on a cold floor. Not when the headache is worse than I want to admit. I try anyway though. I close my eyes, think of Kinsley and hope dreaming of her will be enough to lull me into a deep sleep.

I let the image of her standing in front of me when I thought she was dead fill my mind. I see her standing there, strong and unbreakable, in her tight dark pants that show off the curve of her ass. I let my mind move up her body to her bare stomach, smooth and perfect. Up to her bra that shows off her perky breasts that fit so perfectly in my hands. To her hair that somehow still shines, despite not being styled in days. To her plump lips that I want to claim with mine.

I imagine a different meeting. A meeting where the second I see her, I run to her and never let her go. I run to her, and I don't ask questions about what she is doing here or who she has become. I just take her in my arms and love her.

I imagine ripping her clothes off and not caring who is watching because I need to be with her more than anything. I imagine her moans at the first touch of my hand on her bare breast. I imagine her screaming my name as I thrust inside her, expanding her, until she is more than full. I can practically feel her wetness covering my cock, more and more with each thrust. I feel the tight walls of her pussy contracting as I make her come hard and fast. I hear her screaming, but as soon as she gets the release out, it turns into barely a whisper that she repeats over and over, like a quiet plea for more.

"Killian...Killian...Killian," she says in her soft, perfect voice.

I moan softly, loving how she says my name.

"Killian," she says louder.

I grin wildly as she begs me for more, even when I know she isn't ready for another round so quickly after we just finished.

"Open your eyes, baby," she says softly to me.

I moan. I can't open my eyes. If I do, she will be gone. I'm not ready to let the image go.

"Open your eyes," she says again. This time, she's stroking my cheek so softly that I'm not sure if she is actually touching me.

I begrudgingly open my eyes and expect her to disappear, but instead, I find her crouching in front of me. Her brow is wrinkled as she looks at me, biting down on her lip.

I look around the room and realize I'm still in the prison they locked me in, except Kinsley isn't just an image of my imagination. She is kneeling down in front of me.

I reach my hand to touch her face, but the rope keeps my hand in place. I can't help but smile at her, even though I know she is risking her life to be here.

"You shouldn't be here," I say.

"I couldn't stay away." She reaches her hand up and gently touches me on the cheek.

It stings wherever she touches, but I don't tell her to stop. I can't tell her to stop. I need her touch too much to let a little pain get in the way.

"I'm sorry," she says as she stops rubbing my cheek.

"Don't stop."

My eyes meet hers, and I see a tear fall down her cheek. A tear I can't wipe away, despite how much I need to.

She slowly reaches her hand back to my cheek and touches me so softly that all I feel is the pleasure from her touch.

"I'm so sorry I hit you. I didn't know what else to do. I just couldn't kill you. I couldn't live if you were dead. I'm sorry I kissed Nacio. It was the only thing I could think of. I would have done anything to gain his trust and keep you alive. I couldn't kill you. I couldn't kill you," she says as her voice turns to sobs.

"Shh," I say, cursing the ropes for not letting me touch her. "Stop it. You have nothing to be sorry for, princess. Nothing at all."

She wipes the tears, but as soon as she does, more tears fall. "Yes, I do. I hurt you. I never wanted to hurt you. Ever."

I sigh. "You didn't hurt me tonight. Seeing you alive brought me back from the brink of death. That's all I care about. That you are happy and alive even if..." I can't bear to say the next words. *Even if you don't love me anymore. Even if you never did.*

She stops crying immediately and looks up at me. "You think I hate you, don't you?"

I can't look at her, so instead, I look at the cold, dark ground. I can't answer her. I don't want her to pretend she doesn't hate me when she does.

I feel her hand reach around to the nape of my neck. She slightly lifts my head, forcing me to look at her. She bites her lip again as she looks into my eyes, trying to read my expression, but in my swollen state, I don't think she is able to read any of my emotions.

She pauses for a second longer, studying me, trying to understand, and then her lips are on my lips. Her tongue is in my mouth. Her hand is tangled in my hair. Her kiss demands me to kiss her back, and I oblige as best as I can. I push my tongue further into her mouth until it is tangling with hers. She moans loudly as I do, and as she deepens the kiss, I know there is no way she hates me. There is no way she could feel anything other than love for me. And I hate myself for doubting that love. I hate myself that one word —*never*—made me think that she hated me when I read the note she left in the bed and breakfast in Ireland.

She slowly, reluctantly moves her lips from mine. She places her cheek against my cheek. "I love you. I could never hate you. I love you. I've always loved you. I always will," she says.

"I know, princess. I know. I love you always, too."

She kisses me hard against my cheek, holding the kiss for a long time, like she is preparing to say good-bye, but she isn't. She is just leaning away from my face so we can look at each other again, eye-to-eye.

"You should go." I force the words out of my mouth even though it is the absolute last thing I want.

"I can't. I need you too much first."

I suck in a breath, not able to stand the torture she is putting me through when she promises me something that can't happen. I close my eyes, trying to break the connection between us. "You have to go. I need you to stay alive."

"I will. I will stay alive, but I won't without having you first."

I shake my head and keep my eyes closed, ignoring what she is telling me she wants.

"It's not safe, Kinsley. There are cameras everywhere. There are guards. They can't find you in here. You need to go. I need to know that you are safe. That you are alive."

Her lips touch mine, and I can't keep my eyes closed anymore. They open automatically as she runs her tongue across my bottom lip. I could let her suck me. I could let her fuck me. I wouldn't last. It would be over in a matter of seconds. I've missed her too much to last longer than that.

"No," I say sternly. "No."

"I am safe. I told Karp."

I narrow my eyes in confusion at the name.

"The man who is on guard duty. I told him I wasn't done with you. That I needed to make you pay for what you did. I needed to make sure you weren't hiding anything else. He thinks I'm in here, torturing you, beating you up. There are no cameras in here. We are safe."

"Thank fucking God."

She smiles brightly at me, but the brightness soon fades as more blood drips down my face. She moves closer to me, and I freeze as I watch her tongue move out of her mouth. I anticipate her running it across my lip again, but this time, it moves to the corner of my lip where blood is spilling. She slowly, hesitantly licks up the blood, and I can't do anything but stare at how sexy she is as she laps up the blood.

I can't grab ahold of her with my hands, but it doesn't matter because I grab her lips with my mouth and pull her into mine. I suck hard, tasting the mix of my blood and her in my mouth. Nothing could taste sweeter than the taste of us together.

She suddenly pulls away, far enough away that I can't pull her back in with my lips, and I hate that I'm tied up. She keeps her eyes closed, most likely reliving the kiss, just like I am.

She opens them, and I see the somberness that has formed there.

"What?"

"I need you, but the only way I can have you is if they think I am hurting you. I can only have you if they think I am torturing you."

I nod. "Then damage me, torture me. I would do anything if it meant I got one more chance to love you."

"I'm not sure I can though. I don't think I can hurt you again."

"You can only harm me by walking away and not giving me what I need."

"What do you need?"

"You. I need you."

She thinks for a moment, and then I can see her desire for me overtake any reluctance at the thought of causing me more pain.

"Go get the whip in the corner."

She turns from me and looks reluctantly in the direction where I nod. She doesn't move. She just tucks a strand of hair behind her ear.

"Go."

She slowly walks over and picks up the whip that brought me so much pain earlier at the hands of Seth. And, now, it will bring me pleasure because it means I get to have her.

She picks it up, and it looks awkward in her hand. I know I'm going to have to convince her it's okay for her to wound me. It's more than okay. It's what I want.

My eyes turn dark with desire for her to claim me. My throat turns dry as I think of her taking me. My cock stirs as I think of her riding me, destroying me for any other woman in the world.

She slowly walks back with the whip in her hand. She looks up at my tied-up hands with tears forming in her eyes.

"At least let me untie you."

She walks to my hands and tries to untie me, but I know it's no use. She won't be able to untie the knots—not without spending hours doing so, and that's time we don't have.

"No."

Her hands freeze midair. "Why not?"

I shake my head. "I don't want you to untie me. I want you to hurt me. I want you to dominate me. I want you to make me pay for ever letting you go."

She steps back for a second, and I see her lust for me

grow as she looks into my eyes to see I am telling her the truth.

"You're wet for me, aren't you?"

She sucks in a breath.

"You're wet for me at just the thought of hitting me."

She bites her lip.

"You've had this fantasy before. You've always wanted to be in power. In control."

I watch a tinge of anger mix with her lust.

"But I never let you have control. Take it. Take control now."

I watch as the whip twitches in her hand, begging her to use it.

"Hit me. Claim me. Make me pay for lying to you. For not telling you the truth."

"Don't tell me what to do."

I smirk. I've gotten through. "Then, make up your mind already."

She hits me with the whip, and I feel the sting of it as it hits my exposed stomach.

My smirk widens. "Is that all you've got? I thought you wanted to claim me. I thought you wanted to punish me for what I put you through."

She hits me again, and this time, I feel the passion behind the whip as it hits my thigh.

"Stop talking. I'm the one in control."

She uses the whip again, and I feel it hard against my shoulder.

"You don't get to be in control anymore. Not after you lied to me again and again."

She walks forward and slaps my cheek hard with her other hand, causing me to moan loudly as my wound from her original hit re-opens.

But she makes up for the hit by grabbing my chin and forcing me to kiss her hard and fast until we are both panting.

When she releases me, she hits me square on the other cheek, and a grunt escapes my lips.

She smiles. "How does it feel, not having any control?"

She slides the end of the whip down my face, over my lips, and to my bare chest.

My eyes darken, begging for more, at her seductive speech.

"Princess, I'm not going to last if you don't take me soon."

She shakes her head. "You're not in control. I am."

I feel the sting of the whip hit my back, making me bleed, I'm sure of it. She doesn't know my back is already covered in sores from being whipped before. And I don't let her know. She needs to do this. She needs to injure me to stay safe, and I love letting her hurt me. I love letting her love me.

Her eyes drop to my pants. My jail jumpsuit barely hangs off my hips, and my cock presses against the thin material, begging her to touch me.

I watch with wide eyes as she lets the whip trail down my body until it is just over my cock.

"Don't," I say, my voice a little shaky.

She smiles and then lifts the whip above her head.

I squeeze my eyes closed, afraid of where she is going to hit me. I cry out when she hits me the hardest she has yet, but she doesn't hit my cock. She hits the inside of my thigh. It somehow electrifies me and makes me want her even more.

I open my eyes and am rewarded by a naked Kinsley. My eyes grow wide at the sight of her naked before me. I strain my arms in the ropes, hoping I can get out of them because I need to touch her so fucking bad.

She smiles, watching me squirm. She takes a second longer to run her hand down her body, across her swollen breast and down to her pussy.

I watch in anticipation as she moves her fingers in circles around her clit and her eyes fill with lust. I can no longer breathe when her fingers dip inside her dripping pussy. I can't think. It's the sexiest thing she has ever done.

Her grin grows larger as she sees me lose control when I suddenly call out her name.

She immediately takes the whip and hits me again. My moan turns from pleasure to pain so if anybody were listening in, they would hear her torturing me instead of loving me.

Her hand reaches down and touches my cock through the thin material of the jumpsuit, and I know I'm going to need her to hurt me a lot more if I'm going to cry out in pain instead of love.

I bite my lip, trying to hold back a moan.

"Hurt me," I whisper. "Make it so every time I move tomorrow, I'll think of you. I need more pain if I'm going to make it through this."

Her eyes intensify at my words. She releases me and walks back to the corner of the room. When she returns she has something behind her body, but I can't see what it is.

"Close your eyes," she whispers softly into my ear when she reaches me.

I hesitate for a second, realizing how much trust it takes for me to close my eyes. I do it though. I close my eyes and wait for the sting. It doesn't come though—at least initially.

Instead, I feel cold metal moving across my body. I feel her hand on my cock again, firmly gripping it. I bite my lip, causing more blood to spill out from the corner of my lip, to keep from calling out her name again.

And then I feel the greatest mix of pain and pleasure I have ever felt. I feel cold metal spikes drive hard into my back at the same time as when I feel her claim me with her pussy, straddling over me.

I scream loudly. Loud enough I'm sure the whole building can hear me. It's a painful scream, but at the same time, it's a beautiful scream. It's a scream that makes me love her even more because she knows so perfectly what we both need.

Her hand grabs ahold of my back as she begins moving up and down my thick cock, making the pain a faint memory until it is almost gone.

The second she feels the pain disappearing from me, she grabs my back, digging her nails into the sores on my back while picking up speed.

I scream again, but then she muffles my screams with her mouth as she kisses away the pain.

She picks up speed, and I match her. We both lose control together. We both moan together. We both claim each other.

When we are done, Kinsley grabs ahold of my body, and I know she's exhausted from what she just did. And I know it is going to take everything I have left to convince her to let me go.

I kiss her on the top of her head as my eyes grow heavy again. I need to close them. I need to get some rest. And she does, too.

"Get dressed, princess."

I nudge her with my head, and she stirs a little.

"Get dressed," I say again.

She slowly lets me go and gets dressed. Then, she moves

back to my cock. Her eyes stay on mine, and I nod. She licks my cock clean while I do my best to stay quiet so nobody hears me.

She then pulls my pants back up to where they were.

"You need to go."

She nods this time, and it rips me apart to know this might be the last time I see her. Tomorrow, one of us might be dead.

"Do I look thoroughly beaten up?" I ask, trying to joke with her.

She glances down at my body, and I see the sadness return in her eyes, giving me my answer.

"Hey, it's going to be okay. You're going to survive this."

She shakes her head. "I don't want to survive without you."

"You have to. You have to survive."

"No, I will only survive if you do."

I try to speak again to tell her she has to survive, but she holds a finger up to my lips, silencing me.

"Tomorrow. They are moving everyone to a different location tomorrow."

"Where?"

"I don't know. They don't trust me enough to tell me yet." She pauses and then starts again. "My plan is, after we move to the other location and I find out as much info as I can, I will contact the police and the FBI."

"How?"

"They let me keep my cell phone."

I nod. "You should have called them by now. You can't risk waiting."

She shakes her head, and I know why she won't do it now. Her grandfather isn't here. He's at the next location. Most of the people they smuggled have already been moved. Saving them is more important. Setting things right is more important.

"Fine, but you call them as soon as you are moved. Don't wait."

She nods. "I'm not planning on waiting."

She looks down at her hands and then back up at me. "You have to promise me something," she says.

"Anything."

"Promise me if you have a chance to escape, you will take it. You won't wait for me. You will just go."

"No."

She raises her eyebrow. "Promise me. I need to know you are going to live. They are going to make me kill you. I need you to promise the first chance you get, you will run without me."

I take several deep breaths, trying to figure out how I can get out of promising her, but I don't see a way out.

"Killian?"

"I promise," I say even though it's a lie.

She knows I'm lying to her.

"But you have to promise me something, princess. You have to promise me if they make you choose between your life and mine, you will choose your own life. You will shoot me if you have to. You will kill me to survive. Promise me."

A slow tear drips down her cheek, and it kills me I can't comfort her, I can't hold her.

"Promise me?"

"I promise," she says in a whisper. She wipes the tear from her cheek. "I need to go. One last kiss."

She places her lips against mine, and I suck her in, trying my best to make her feel better. Trying my best to take away her pain, but I know the agony remains, just like it remains inside me. We both know this could be our last kiss. Our last touch.

I feel our tears falling down our cheeks and mixing together. Then, suddenly, Kinsley is pulling away.

"Stay alive, princess."

She nods and wipes her eyes.

We don't say anything else to each other. Neither of us can say anything more. We both know we love each other. We both promised we would survive, even at the cost of the other. We both lied.

Kinsley keeps her eyes on me as she walks to the door, and I keep my eyes on her, trying my best to take this memory with me forever. But I'm not sure I can take the memory with me.

I'm afraid, as soon as she walks out the door, I will lose her forever. I'm afraid the pain will return, and I won't survive. But maybe that's for the best. Maybe, if I die, she will live.

12

KINSLEY

I close the door behind me, and I lose all control of my feelings. My emotions all mix together, and I no longer know how I feel. Happy or sad. Hopeful or defeated. Satisfied or longing. Everything mixes the second the door closes to the only person left I truly love.

I look down the hallway to where Karp was sitting earlier, watching guard. He's still sitting there, but his eyes are no longer open. His head is drooped down, and I can hear him snoring from here.

My shoulders relax a little as I see him asleep. I should have a clear shot back to my bedroom. The only person who might see me is whoever is watching the security cameras tonight. That is, if they are awake enough to keep an eye on the screens.

I don't hesitate to wait and see if anybody is going to notice me. Instead, I walk down the long hallway that feels of death to the stairwell. I climb down the stairs to where my bedroom is.

I pull the door open to my room, but the door is slammed shut. My whole body jumps, and my eyes close automatically at the sudden movement. I turn to see who it is, expecting Nacio or Santino. Instead, I find Seth breathing down my neck, just inches from me.

"What were you doing?" he asks.

I cross my arms and give him a stern look. "I was getting my revenge on Killian. I didn't think he had been punished enough. I wanted him to suffer more. I wasn't sure about what you were able to get out of him. I wanted to see what other information he would tell us."

I turn to walk into the room that will be my bedroom for one more night, but Seth doesn't remove his hand from the door. He doesn't allow me access to the room.

"I don't believe you tortured him. I don't believe you could torture anyone. And you aren't supposed to leave your room without permission. It's not allowed."

"Well, I did. Go check him yourself, and you will see."

Seth grabs my arm and pushes me hard against the wall. He pulls a gun out from the waistband of his pants but doesn't aim it at my head. He just casually holds it, letting me know he could use it.

Except he can't use it. Nacio would be pissed. And Seth would be the next one to die.

I smile, looking at the gun. "You aren't going to shoot me. Don't even pretend."

His frown deepens, and his face turns scarlet red. "You don't get to give me orders. Not yet."

I smile wider. "Neither do you. Now, I suggest you let me go to bed if you don't want me to speak to Nacio about your actions."

Seth slowly releases me, still holding his gun by his side.

I walk past him and open the door to take my barracks and walk inside. I quickly close and lock the door behind me, not that it would hold anyone out. I wait at the door, listening silently, until I hear his footsteps walking away. Then, I walk through the dark room to the bunk that I have made into my bed.

I don't notice the smell anymore. I don't notice the dirt on the floor or the stains on the bed.

I don't even think about Seth. I don't think about the fact that he will report my actions to Nacio. I don't think about the fact that Nacio could kill me before I even have a chance to explain.

All I think about is Killian. I think about how it felt to have his muscles flexing beneath me. I think about how his lips devoured mine. I think about how his cock claimed me. I wish those were all the things I could think about. But along with the most pleasurable moments with Killian also come the most painful.

My body shakes as I remember seeing Killian tied up. His body was obviously broken from torture. His heart was broken at the thought that I no longer loved him.

That is what destroyed me worse than seeing any of the painful marks that crossed his body. I hate I was the one who caused him so much misery.

I hate I had to use the whip to bring him more injuries so we could both experience pleasure. Somehow though, the sting of the whip brought us closer together instead of further apart. I don't understand why, but I enjoyed the power the whip gave me over Killian. Torturing him turned me on. The power turned me on. I was afraid hurting him would make him hate me, but instead, it made him just as excited as I was.

If we both survive this, I will have to remember to bring more excitement into the bedroom. The only problem is, I don't think we will both survive tomorrow, let alone live long enough to experiment more with whips, canes, and bondage.

I try to push Killian out of my head. I try to think of anything else, but my thoughts keep coming back to him. I lie down on the bed, trying my best to sleep.

But I can't sleep. If I sleep, I'm afraid my dreams will be of the girl who died. Or of what Nacio said about Killian killing my father. Or I'll dream of having to kill Killian.

So, I won't dream. I won't sleep. I can't. Instead, I will just relive my last night with Killian over and over and pretend tomorrow will never come.

———

"Pull the trigger," Nacio says.

I hold the gun in my hand, but I don't understand why I would pull the trigger. Why would I want to kill anyone?

"Kill him. He killed your father. Kill him."

His words anger me. I want nothing more than to kill whoever killed my father. I loved my father. No matter what he did, he didn't deserve to die. I turn toward the man kneeling on the ground.

Killian.

"I can't kill him," I say.

"Yes, you can. Kill him. Pull the trigger. Gain our trust."

"No."

"Kill him, or we will kill you."

"No."

"It's you or him."

Tears threaten, but I don't let them out.

"Choose now."

I look at Killian, who nods, giving me permission to kill him.

I pull the trigger...

————

"Wake up, sweetheart. It's time to go."

I open my eyes and try to remain calm, but I can't stop my chest from rising and falling way too fast. I can't stop the panting or hide the sweat on my face.

I sit up, wiping the perspiration off my forehead caused by the dream I'm too afraid will become my reality.

"You okay, sweetheart?" Nacio asks.

I yawn, trying to calm my speeding heart. "I'm fine. Just thrown from being woken up so early in the morning."

"It's time to go."

"Go where?"

Nacio just smiles and walks away.

I groan and stretch before I get out of bed. I couldn't have slept more than an hour or two. I tried not to sleep, but somehow, sleep must have found me.

I rub my arms, feeling cold. I stand and walk to the bed across from mine where I piled up my clothes. I dig through the clothes, trying to find something suitable to wear. Something that won't make me feel like a complete slut.

I don't find anything. I change my bra into a white crop top that might as well be a bra. I grab the jacket Santino lent to me. I slip it on and then walk out into the hallway where Nacio is waiting for me.

He frowns when he sees the jacket. "Where did you get that?"

I shrug and yawn again. "Where are we going?"

"To our next base of operations."

I swallow hard, trying to calm my nerves creeping back up again. I don't know where the next place is or what it holds, which is what scares me the most.

"Let's go," Nacio says, holding out his arm to me.

I ignore it.

"Shouldn't I pack my clothes and things first?"

"No, I'll have the other men pack up your clothing and bring it when they come. We have a flight to catch."

I nod.

Nacio waits a second longer for me to grab ahold of his arm. When I don't grab ahold of it, he sighs and then walks to the stairwell. I follow. We climb down the stairs without saying a word before I realize I don't have my purse with my phone in it.

"One second, I need to go back to grab my purse."

"We don't have time."

"I'll be just a second. My passport is in there."

"You won't need a passport."

"We aren't leaving the country?"

"We are, but you don't need a passport."

"I would like to have my phone and IDs."

Nacio grabs my arm and leads me to the exit of the building. "We don't have time, and like I said before, you won't need them. We will make sure you have everything you need once we get there."

I want to protest again, but I don't. My phone was the only way I had to contact the outside world. It was my security to call in the police if I got desperate. Now, I have nothing.

I walk outside, happy to taste some fresh air after being stuck inside the building for days. It is still dark outside, making me suspect even more that it is very early in the morning. My best guess is three or four. The only sound I hear is the gentle humming of the two vans parked outside the building. The windows on both of the vans are dark, making it impossible to see inside.

Nacio opens the door to the first van. "Ladies first," he says to me, holding the door open for me.

I climb into the van and notice Seth and Santino are already sitting in the backseat. I take the middle, and Nacio climbs in after me.

A man I don't recognize climbs into the front seat and quickly begins driving. The car ride is silent. I suspect everyone is too tired to be up for any conversation.

I lean my head against the van window and watch the broken, old buildings roll by. The buildings quickly turn from broken down to shiny, new hotels that make up most of the city.

Nacio slings his arm around my shoulders. I turn and glare at him, but he isn't looking at me. His head is resting against the headrest with his eyes closed. I sigh and surrender to having his arm around my shoulders for the rest of the van ride.

I'm tempted to close my own eyes as we drive. My eyes grow heavy with each sway of the van, but I can't close my eyes. Not with Seth in the back. At any moment, he might decide to tell Nacio or Santino of my actions last night. If I fall asleep, I could dream of Killian, and I can't take the chance I might talk in my sleep. So, I don't sleep. I stay awake as the van drives and drives.

The van slows as we reach an airport. I assume the driver will stop out front and drop us off. He doesn't though. He drives up to a metal gate. I watch as he rolls down his window.

A man speaks in barely audible Spanish over the speaker, but it must be audible enough to our driver because he says, "The Marlows are here."

A loud buzzer sounds, waking up Nacio. The gate opens, and the driver rolls us through and onto the tarmac of the airport. We drive a little farther, and then the van parks in front of a large private plane. My mouth drops as I realize this is how we are flying.

I've flown private several times before with my father, but I guess I didn't think a bunch of criminals would fly privately. It makes sense though, as there would be less questions. But, even with the size of the plane, I know the number of men I saw earlier will not fit on the plane. They also won't fit in the two vans that drove us here.

I turn to Nacio. "How are the rest of the men getting to wherever we are going? They won't all fit on the plane, will they?"

He studies me for a second and then opens the door. "No, they won't fit," he says as he climbs out of the car.

I quickly climb out after him, not satisfied with his answer. "Then, how are they getting there?"

"They aren't."

"What do you mean?"

"They are staying behind for the FBI to find."

I raise my eyebrows, not fully understanding. "Alive or..."

He smirks at me and then softly pats me on the cheek, like I'm a child. He doesn't answer. Instead, he walks over to the plane and climbs the stairs, leaving me standing on the tarmac alone.

But I have my answer. The men that I saw and had dinner with. The men whom I realized were just ordinary men. Nothing more or less, just trying to survive. Most of them are now dead or will be.

Santino grabs my arm, bringing me back to the present. "Come on. You won't get a good seat on the plane if you don't."

I smile and follow Santino onto the plane. The inside of

the plane is large. Larger than most of the private planes I have been on before. The first area is made to look like a living room. Two large couches that could easily hold half a dozen men line each side of the living room. A flat screen TV sits in the corner. I walk past the living room and find a large bar already stocked full with food and drinks.

Past the bar is a business area with individual recliners, tables, and TVs. I count six large recliners. Past the recliners is a bathroom door and a second door, which leads to a bedroom, if I had to guess.

I'm not sure where I should sit—the living area or the reclining chairs in the business area. If I had my choice, it would be the large reclining chairs in the business area.

"Sit anywhere but the first on the left. That's Nacio's seat," Santino says.

I smile at Santino and then take a chair on the right, far away from where Santino said Nacio would be sitting. Santino smiles back at me and then takes the reclining chair in front of me. The chair I'm in gives a great view of the entire aircraft. I can see the bar, living room area, and even the edge of the cockpit.

I lean back, loving how comfortable the chair is. I plan on sleeping most of the flight to wherever we are going. I recline the chair, put my feet up, and close my eyes, preparing to do just that.

"What are you doing?" Nacio asks.

"Sleeping." I open my eyes and see Nacio standing over me with a frown on his face.

"Oh, leave her alone," Santino says, reclining his own chair. "She just wants to sleep. If you want to sit by her so bad, sit in that chair there instead of your usual chair." Santino nods to the chair just across the aisle from me.

Nacio's frown deepens, but he takes a seat across the

aisle from me instead of where Santino says he usually sits. I sigh. I wanted to sit alone, but instead, I'm surrounded by the Marlow men.

I begin to close my eyes again when I hear more men getting on board. Men I don't recognize. I wait to find the men that I do know. I wait to see Karp or Raul climb on. But I don't see them. I watch as all the men fill the couches up front.

The only person I know left is Seth, as far as I see. I glance across the aisle and see Nacio pulling a computer out of his bag. I glance the other way and find Santino is already snoring.

I relax a little, hoping they won't bother me during the flight, so I will be able to get some sleep just as long as Seth takes the one remaining seat on the couches up front.

I close my eyes, trying to drift off, when I hear Seth's voice.

"Where do you want him, sir?" Seth asks.

I open my eyes and find Killian standing in front of me with Seth behind him, holding on to Killian's shoulder. Killian looks bad. Worse than the last time I saw him. He's still wearing the same jumpsuit he was wearing before, but it is now covered in dirt and blood. His chest is exposed, as the top half of the suit is torn. His chest is covered in whip marks, blood, dirt, and sweat. Marks I caused.

I feel a tinge in my chest at the sight of him in such a state. His arms are tied behind his back. I take a chance and look into his eyes that have deep circles under them from lack of sleep. His hair is matted on top of his head. Tape covers his mouth, but I still see a trickle of blood fall from a corner onto the stubble covering his chin and neck.

Still, even his current state doesn't stop the desire from creeping up inside me. I want nothing more than to take him into the back room of the plane and fuck him until we are both satisfied. Even though I just had him last night, it wasn't enough. It will never be enough. No matter how many times I have him, I will always want more.

Killian doesn't look at me. Instead, he looks at Nacio. I want him to look at me though. I need to see the love is still there. I need to see he still has fight left. That he hasn't given up yet. That he is going to live. But he doesn't look at me.

It doesn't keep me from staring at him. Even though I have to look at him with anger and disgust, I still stare because I can't *not* look at his strong body I fell in love with.

Nacio stands as he glances past him to the front of the plane and then sighs. "Put him in one of the chairs there," Nacio says, pointing to his usual chair.

Seth tugs on Killian's arm and shoves him into the chair. He buckles Killian in, so he can't move. The chair is facing forward, away from me, so I can barely see him unless he intentionally turns his head around. He won't. He's too worried someone will find out about what I did last night. So, he won't look at me. Instead, he will face forward and pretend he hates me.

I watch as Seth takes a seat behind Killian and in front of Nacio. Now, I won't be able to sleep. I can't leave Seth alone to talk with Nacio. I hope Seth will sleep himself so I can get some rest. But he seems intent on making sure Killian doesn't move. Not that there will be anywhere for Killian to go as soon as the plane takes off.

I close my eyes as the pilot comes over the intercom, telling us to buckle our seat belts and how long the flight will be. I don't listen, despite knowing the pilot could be telling me where we are going. I can't focus on anything other than Killian. I can't focus on anything other than the fact that whether or not I pull the trigger, I'm the reason Killian is going to die.

The plane takes off, and I know Killian and I's time is limited. Every second we get closer to our next location is one second less that Killian has to live. I must find a way to keep him alive. I have an entire plane ride to form a plan and to find any reason that he should live. I saved him once from death. I'm just not sure I can find a way to do it again.

13

KILLIAN

The chair feels like heaven, despite my hands being tied behind my back. I am able to rest my head on the headrest, and even though I can't recline the chair unless Seth reclines it for me, I am still able to get some sleep I desperately need.

Sleep might be the only thing that keeps me from thinking about Kinsley. The only thing that will keep my eyes away from hers. The only way to keep our love hidden.

I close my eyes, expecting sleep to come easily, but then I hear Nacio speak, and I know I won't be able to sleep.

"Paris," Nacio simply says.

"What?" Kinsley's beautiful voice asks.

I force my head forward instead of looking in her direction.

"We are going to Paris. I think it's safe to tell you now. You'll find out anyway as soon as we land."

"Really? Paris?"

"You sound shocked." He laughs. "It seems your grandfather found the perfect place to continue our work in plain sight, so we don't have to hide in a dark, abandoned building, like we did in Mexico." He pauses. "When we get there, we should go to dinner. I know the perfect place to take you. Of course, we will have to wait until after you pass the final test."

My heart beats rapidly in my chest. I won't be able to stand it if she says yes, but I know that is what she should say. Thank God I'm tied up. Otherwise, I would beat that man for even asking her out.

"That would be nice," she says sweetly.

I can hear the hesitation in her voice. I just hope no one else can tell she's hesitating. I hope no one else understands the disgust in her voice.

I'm glad it's Paris though and not another dark, dank city with no way for her to escape. If they are in the heart of a city, she will have a chance to live.

I close my eyes again when they stop talking, hoping everyone will settle in for the long flight. But, of course, that doesn't happen.

"Sir, I need to speak with you about an incident I saw on the security cameras last night," Seth says.

I freeze, knowing he is talking about Kinsley entering my room. My hands begin trying to untie the rope I know won't come untied, but it doesn't keep me from trying. My only hope is they won't kill Kinsley on the plane. I have to hope they will keep her alive at least until we reach Paris. By then, I might have a plan to keep her alive.

Nacio sighs. "Not here, Seth. If any of the men were involved, it can't be properly dealt with here."

"It doesn't involve the men," Seth says.

"Well, everyone else is dead or shipped off. I don't need to know the details."

"It involved Kinsley."

"Thank you, Seth, but I can tell the story from here. Like I said last night, it doesn't involve you," Kinsley says.

"I disagree. I think it does involve me," Seth says.

"I—" Kinsley says.

"What did you see, Seth?" Nacio says, silencing Kinsley.

"Kinsley decided to visit the FBI agent last night. She stayed for almost an hour and then went back to her room. When I saw her leaving his room, I approached her and questioned her. She said she was there to torture him more, but I don't believe her."

"Is that true, sweetheart?" Nacio asks.

"Yes, I went to see Killian." Her voice strengthens with each word. "I went to see him because I didn't think he had fully paid for what he did to my father. And I wanted more information. I wanted him to tell me why he'd killed my father. I wanted to find out if he was still hiding something."

"I don't think that's why she visited him, sir. I think she still loves him. I don't think we can trust her, sir," Seth says.

"Look at him! Look at Killian! His body is completely broken after what I did to him, and I still don't think it is enough. He hasn't suffered a fraction for what he has done. I should have killed him. I shouldn't have let him live."

"Sir—" Seth starts.

"Enough, Seth. It doesn't matter what Kinsley went in there for. It's obvious Killian has more wounds than he did before. All that matters is Kinsley kills him when it matters."

"But—" Seth tries to speak.

"Enough, Seth. Go check on the pilots to make sure we are still going to land on time."

I watch Seth get up and walk past me with a grim look on his face.

And then I hear Kinsley scream, and it takes every nerve

in my body not to react to her pain. I can't when I know Nacio and Santino are watching me.

"Get off me!" she screams.

"No, not until you understand your life is in danger. Not until you understand you don't have a choice. You are either with us, or you are dead. You don't get to do whatever the fuck you want. Do you understand?"

"Get off of her. She can't breathe," Santino says, sounding bored.

I hear Kinsley wheeze, and I breathe a little easier myself, knowing Nacio is no longer holding her neck.

"That is your last chance, sweetheart. Fuck up again, and I will kill you," Nacio says.

No other words are spoken, but I can feel the tension between Kinsley and Nacio and even Seth when he returns. Still, none of them speak.

I wait. I wait until most of their breathing has turned back to the calm steadiness it was before, and then I turn my head just enough to see her out of the corner of my eye. I thought she would look weak or scared. She doesn't. She looks strong. She has a plan. I can see it in her eyes as she glances back at me. I just hope her plan involves her living. Because there is no use in saving me if she doesn't save herself.

14

KINSLEY

I'VE FAILED.

I know I've failed. I know Nacio is suspicious. I know I didn't convince him. The marks he left on my neck prove he doesn't believe me, he thinks I still care about Killian.

I've failed. I have no idea how to keep Killian or I alive any longer. We will both die. As soon as I prove I can't kill Killian, Nacio will kill us both.

I pretend to sleep for the rest of the flight, but it is a useless endeavor. I can't sleep. I don't think I will ever be able to sleep again.

I keep my eyes closed until I feel the plane land on the runway. I open them and find everyone else doing the same —slowly opening their eyes. It seems everyone was pretending to sleep rather than talk to each other. Or they were actually sleeping.

No one speaks as the plane pulls to a stop outside the Paris airport. I watch as the men at the front of the plane disembark. I watch as Seth exits the plane and then climbs back on. I watch him unbuckle Killian from the recliner chair. I watch Killian stand, and I see the bruises and lacerations covering his back. He doesn't glance back at me as much as I know he wants to. Instead, he walks forward, away from me. I try to look away, but I can't. My eyes stay on him until the last second when he walks off the plane.

I watch as Santino stands and begins exiting the plane, leaving me alone with Nacio. I stand, but Nacio grabs ahold of my arm, preventing me from moving off the plane.

I look at him, but the look in his eyes scares me. His eyes look red instead of their usual shade of green. All of the muscles in his face are pulled tight as he glares at me. He's going to kill me before I even have a chance to speak with my grandfather. Before I even have a chance to run to a phone and tell the FBI about our new location. He's going to kill me right here on this plane.

"I know your secret."

I suck in a breath, but I try to remain calm and not give anything away.

"I don't have anything to hide."

"Yes, you do. Since you first came here, I've suspected your intentions weren't pure. I'm still not entirely sure what your intentions are. But I do know you care about the FBI agent more than you should, so you can stop trying to hide it.

"I no longer care about how you currently feel. I care about how you *will* feel. What future you will choose. I intend to show you what you could have if you choose me, if you choose a life of running the company your father cared so much about. If you choose me over him."

"And if I don't?"

"You already know what will happen to you." He strokes my neck, still sore from where he choked me. "You will both die instead of just him."

He releases my arm, but I don't move. I watch as he

picks up his bag and stands. He smiles at me as he grabs my hand and leads me off the plane. I let him.

He's giving me more time, I realize as we get off the plane. He doesn't want to force me to kill Killian. He wants me to *want* to kill Killian. He wants me to want to choose him over Killian. So, I have to make him think I'm open to the idea of being with him.

When I glance up I expect to see another crummy van waiting to pick us up like before, but I guess we only ride in luxury in Paris as a black luxury sedan is waiting. I climb into the backseat and see Santino already sitting in the front. Nacio climbs in after me. This time, when he puts his arm around me, I lean into him just the slightest, enough that I smell his cologne. It is much too strong, suffocating me with the stench. But I don't move away as much as my nose wants me to.

I glance out the window and notice two vans driving away. One of them must contain Killian. I try not to stare or think about him. I just try to pretend I'm open to giving Nacio a chance.

The driver begins driving off the tarmac. The ride is beautiful. I watch historic buildings pass us by as we drive to the heart of the city. We pass buildings I have been in several times while on trips here with my father. We pass restaurants. We pass the Eiffel Tower. We pass the Louvre. We pass everything that everyone cares about so much in this city.

It all seems so beautiful. I would give anything to go back in time and enjoy everything more. The food, the history, the people—I would have enjoyed all of it more. Appreciated all of it more.

But, now that I know a base of operations is here, I wonder if every visit here with my father was just another chance for him to smuggle. For him to meet with Nacio's father.

Every time he ran off to take a meeting or phone call, was he really taking a meeting with Nacio? Was he dealing with an employee he had to kill?

Now, every memory I have of him, every single memory I have of traveling the world with him, is tarnished.

The car finally stops outside of a building. Santino jumps out, seemingly happy to spread his legs. Nacio climbs out next and makes his way over to my door. He opens the door to my side of the car, and I climb out.

The warm sun shines down on me as I glance up at the building so typical of Paris. In fact, if I didn't know any better, I feel like I might have stayed at this building before. The building is four stories with white brick walls. Windows are scattered up the front with balconies protruding from each one.

I don't understand how they can smuggle people in a building like this. I don't understand how they think their men could go in and out of this building without others seeing it as suspicious.

I don't think my grandfather, mother, or I could leave this building without being recognized. Not when we are all supposed to be dead.

I follow Nacio into the building, hating that there is such darkness living in such a beautiful place. As I suspected, the inside is just as beautiful as the outside. The entrance is simple, full of white with colorful pops of silk flowers. The building looks like it used to be an apartment building, but now, it runs as our headquarters.

Nacio guides me to a row of doors. He points to the first door. "My office." He points to the second. "Your grandfather's." He points to the third.

"My father's," I say, already knowing the answer.

He nods and then walks to the second door. He knocks loudly on it.

"Come in," my grandfather's voice says.

Nacio pushes the door open, and I walk in behind him. I see my grandfather behind the desk. My eyes widen at the sight. I knew he would be here, but somehow, actually seeing him here makes everything real. It proves to me how horrible he really is.

Granddad looks at me but doesn't really look at me. Instead, he looks through me, like I'm not really here. He turns his attention back to Nacio, who walks over and takes a seat in the chair across from Granddad's desk.

"We have a new shipment coming in an hour. Are your men ready?" my grandfather asks.

"They will be. They are settling in the agent and the last shipment now," Nacio answers.

"Good. We need to discuss what the agent is doing here. That wasn't what we agreed to. He was to be killed and left for the FBI to find tomorrow when they raid our facility," Granddad says sternly. His face is already becoming flushed red.

Nacio pulls out the chair next to him, and I walk over and take the seat, but Granddad still doesn't acknowledge me.

"I realized the plan we discussed was flawed. We needed security, so if we did fuck up and leave a trail for the FBI to our location here, we would have a way out. A way to protect ourselves," Nacio says.

"We shouldn't need a way to protect ourselves! You should have made sure you wouldn't fuck up!" Granddad says.

"It was my decision to make!" Nacio says.

"No, it wasn't!" Granddad stands, his anger overtaking him.

All I can think is, if he keeps this up, he will have another heart attack, but I don't say anything.

"We need to change locations," Granddad says.

"Oh, not this again. We have been in this location for years. It is perfectly safe here. There is no need to move to a different location," Nacio says.

"No! It is not safe here. I've already looked into more suitable locations south of here."

Nacio shakes his head. "Maybe it's time I buy you out. You've lost your mind, old man. We can't shut down our two main locations, not at the same time. We would never recover."

"This is ridiculous! You don't have the power here. I have the final say, and you know it."

"No, you don't. That's where you are wrong. You don't have any more power than I do. Not now that Robert is gone."

Granddad glares at Nacio. "Perhaps it's time we go our separate ways then."

"Indeed, it is time. It is time for you to go, since that is what you want so much. The Marlows will continue running things here."

Granddad snarls at Nacio while Nacio leans back in his chair with a smug grin on his face.

"What are you doing here?" my mother's shrill voice says from behind me.

I turn slowly in my chair and watch as she glances from me to Nacio and then to Granddad.

"I'm here to run the Felton empire. To gain money and power, same as you."

"You..." She walks to me. "You shouldn't be here. You ruin everything."

"You must not be running a very good business here if one woman could bring down everything," I say.

Her cheeks turn bright red, and I can see the alcohol lingering in her bloodshot eyes. She should be in rehab, not here.

"You'll see, Nacio. You should have killed her when she showed up at your door in Mexico," Mother says before walking back out of the office with a bottle in her hand.

I should cry at my mother's words. I should feel sad or hurt or some sort of pain. I don't though.

I feel free, knowing I had every right to hate my mother all these years. I'm not her daughter, and she is not my mother. I feel a release at knowing I no longer have to feel anything for my mother because I never had a mother.

15

KINSLEY

Nacio glances down at his watch. "I need to go see that the new shipment gets settled." He stands and then turns to me. "Sweetheart?" Nacio waits for me at the door.

"I need to speak with my grandfather."

"You sure? I wouldn't waste your time with him if I were you."

"I'm sure."

I look at Granddad, who is still standing behind his desk, pretending like I'm not even here.

"I'll come find you when we are finished," I say.

I watch Granddad keep his eyes glued on Nacio behind me. When Granddad looks back down at his desk, I assume Nacio has gone.

"I think we have a lot to talk about."

Granddad takes a seat in his desk chair and leans back with his arms crossed in front of his body. His nostrils are flared, and his face is still red with anger. He finally looks up at me. "We have nothing to talk about. You shouldn't be here. You should leave before you get yourself killed."

I frown even though he's right. I probably will get myself killed. He should be protecting me though. He should be telling me he wouldn't let that happen. I don't have a mother, and it seems I never really had a grandfather. Or a father. I never had a family.

"No, I have to be here. I'm here because my family does horrible things. My family kills and rapes and tortures. And I want to be a part of it.

"I no longer have a life at home. You ruined it. If I go home, I'll be thrown in jail. My only hope for a real life is here, ensuring the family legacy lives on."

Granddad laughs. "You won't survive here. You would have more of a life in jail than here. Leave before you are too far in to be able to leave."

I raise my eyebrows. "No. You won't let me anyway. I already know too much to be able to leave. I want to do this. I want to understand my father. I want to work with the only family I have left."

Granddad runs his hand through his hair. "You can't do this work. You aren't suited for it. It will kill you if you try."

"It will kill me if I don't." I tuck my hair behind my ear. "I want to know the truth. And I want to be given a chance to be a part of the organization."

Granddad laughs again. "What makes you think I would let you help run this organization when I wouldn't even let you run the legal part of the Felton Corporation?"

"Because I don't think it's up to you to decide."

He frowns. "You think it's up to Nacio?" He laughs. "That boy isn't much better than you are. No, the decision is mine to make." He stands from his desk and walks to me. "You are right about one thing. You are in too deep now for us to simply let you go. You want to be a part of this organization? Then, prove it."

My eyes widen. I'm afraid I've woken a sleeping giant. I'm afraid he will take me to Killian right away to put a bullet in his head. I shouldn't have provoked Granddad.

I just want to understand why my family does this. I just want to find out the truth of what they do and how. As soon as I do, I'll make the call to the police, and this will be over.

I stand and follow Granddad out of the office. He walks to the elevator and presses the button. I should stand and wait and let him tell me whatever it is he wants to tell me, but I can't. I'm done waiting.

"I want answers. I want to know why. How? I think I deserve to know after everything you have put me through."

Granddad doesn't seem fazed by my questions. Instead, an elevator arrives and he walks in, pressing the button for the second floor. "Why is simple. We needed money to start the casinos."

The doors open to the second floor, and Granddad steps out and stops just outside of the elevator.

I follow him. "Why did it continue though after you got the money for the casinos?"

"We were hooked. The money was better and easier than anything the casinos could provide. We were good at it. The casinos were just a front and a means to find what we needed."

I scrunch my nose.

"What did you need?"

Granddad smiles. "You already know the answer to that."

"People to smuggle."

He nods. "People, drugs, diamonds. Anything of value, we learned to smuggle and make a profit. The casinos simply provided us with a large group of people to choose from to smuggle and sell."

I think back to a conversation I had with the executives at the Felton Grand casino after Granddad left. I remember something about employees not showing up to work. My eyes widen as I realize how they find the people. "You smuggled people from our casinos. That's why employees didn't show up to work. That's why guests disappeared unexpectedly. You were taking them."

"Just the ones without family. Just the ones who wouldn't be missed."

"Then, how are you going to find people to smuggle now?"

He smiles. "The same way we always have. Just because I'm not there in person doesn't mean we can't continue to find people and drugs from the casinos. But those aren't the only places we find them. We have our hands in various corporations involved in helping us find and sell them."

Them. I hate how casually he says the word. I hate how casually he speaks of ruining people's lives.

"Who do we sell the drugs and...people to?" I force the words out of my mouth.

"Mainly men with money. Men who want to party and have a good time without having to deal with the laws of everyday society."

"So, for sex? You sell the women to men for sex."

He nods. "Usually."

Granddad begins walking again, and I follow a step behind. He walks purposefully down the hallway and then turns right into a large room that most likely used to be a recreation room of some sort when the building was an apartment building.

There aren't any furniture or decorations in this room. The room is empty with scuffed white walls, except for a pole in the center that I can't keep my eyes off of. The pole has bloodstains dripping off of it, bearing the pain of who knows how many men, women, and children over the years. I don't know what it is for, but I have an idea.

I don't know why Granddad has brought me to the empty room. *To show me what they do to those who disobey? Or is he planning on tying me to the pole and beating me himself?*

I don't ask. I can be patient. I can wait. Because I don't like any of the answers he might tell me. I can't come up with one single answer that would bring me any peace.

I look up at Granddad, who is typing something on his phone.

"I should go find Nacio," I say as I begin to walk out of the room that scares me half to death.

"No. Nacio will be joining us shortly."

"Why?" I ask the question I have been avoiding.

"If you are going to stay here, I need to know which side you are on. You can't be on the Marlows' side. You are a Felton. You must be loyal to the Feltons."

"Why should I when all the Feltons ever did to me was lie?"

"Because, like it or not, you are a Felton, not a Marlow."

"What if I became a Marlow?"

Granddad raises his eyebrows at me. "I don't think you will."

"I might. The Marlows have treated me better than my own family ever has."

"Even if you married one of them, it wouldn't change anything. You were born a Felton. You don't have a choice."

"Here's the man who raped the woman," Nacio says suddenly from behind us without any warning.

I turn my attention from Granddad to Nacio. My mouth drops when I see Karp standing in front of him. I didn't think he had even made the trip. I thought he was dead in Mexico.

"Good. Make an example of him," Granddad says.

"My pleasure," Nacio says, smiling.

He begins walking Karp over to the pole in the center of the room. He locks eyes with me, silently begging me to help him. I look back at him but don't tell him anything. I don't know why he thinks I will be able to help him. He's the one who chose to work for these terrible men, even knowing the consequences. He was the one who raped a woman, despite knowing he wasn't allowed to.

I watch as Nacio makes quick work of tying Karp's arms above his head, attaching the rope to a loop at the top of the pole. Karp doesn't even fight him. I think he knows it will be worse if he does, but I can see the terror forming in his eyes.

I look back to the door when I hear more people filing past the room. Woman after woman walks past the room, each with a man who works for Nacio and Granddad. Each man holds on to a woman's arm or the rope tied around the woman's wrists. Each woman looks different yet the same. Most are wearing business-casual clothing, as if they just got off work. Some are wearing workout clothing. Some are just in casual clothes. But all show fear. All look to me with hope, like I'm the one who is strong enough to help them. They don't understand I am just as much a prisoner as they are. My life is just as much at risk.

One woman in particular catches my eye. She looks so normal in her black pants and business jacket. Her hair is dark brown and curled, landing halfway down her back. She doesn't look much older than I am. The only unusual things about her are that her arms are tied tightly together in front of her body and her eyes. Her eyes are wild with anger and fear. She was the one Karp raped without permission.

I don't know what the future holds for this woman. I don't know where they plan to ship her off to or if they will rape or beat her first. But, now that I've seen her, I know I can't let them do it. I can't let them hurt her. I won't be able to live with myself if I do.

I silently promise her I will save her, or at the least I will get the revenge from these men, something she may never get.

I turn back to the door when I see the children walk by next, and my heart stops. They can't be more than seven, eight, or maybe nine years old. All of their arms are also tied with a man holding onto the end of the rope. Each wears a look of fear. Some have tears falling fast down their faces.

The children are what kill me more than anything. Seeing them here, knowing my family has ripped them from theirs and plans to sell them to someone who only sees them as a sex object, it's too much to bear.

I watch until the women and children are gone. To be held in a room until they are sold. It's too much to fathom even though I just saw it with my own eyes.

I glance back to the door and see Killian walking in, looking even more badly beaten than before. Seth holds on to his arm with a gun pointed at his head.

"You'll be next if you don't behave," Seth growls to Killian.

Nacio steps forward with something black in his hand that I can barely see.

Then men who work for Nacio return after locking up the women and children.

"You didn't follow orders, Karp. You touched a woman who wasn't yours. And you don't have the money to buy her. You robbed us of money, and now you will pay."

16

KILLIAN

I STAND UNCOMFORTABLY against the wall. I try to keep my eyes off of Kinsley, but they automatically go there. Her eyes aren't on me though. They are on Karp. She's glaring at him for what he did to that woman. Even though, the woman would have been raped eventually by some man Nacio or her granddad sold her to. I know Kinsley still thinks she will be able to save them, but I'm not even sure if we will be able to save ourselves, let alone anyone else.

She looks strong in the center of the room with her granddad. She is wearing tight jeans and a jacket covering most of her bare stomach, but when she moves, I get a glimpse of it and her lace bra.

I watch as Nacio holds a whip in his hand and walks toward the man in the center of the room. I look closely at it, thinking it is the same whip used on me. The same one Kinsley used on me when she fucked me earlier. But, on closer inspection, I realize it is not the same whip. This whip has small spikes at the end. This whip is meant to inflict the most pain possible.

"You cost us a couple hundred grand when you raped

her, Karp," Nacio says as he walks closer to Karp, firmly gripping the whip. "We could have easily gotten that much for the virgin. Now, we will get less than half for her initial purchase. We should make you pay with that many lashes, but I don't think you would survive, and unfortunately, we don't have the time to break in a new man yet."

Nacio thinks for a minute as he steps forward. "The last man we whipped only lasted thirty lashes before he begged for mercy. We gladly put a bullet between his eyes, releasing him from the pain."

I glance at Karp, the man tied tightly to the pole. Nacio rips his shirt open, exposing his back. I can't see Karp's face as Nacio lifts the whip, but I know it must read fear.

"If you can survive to thirty-five, your debt will be paid."

Nacio brings the whip down hard on the man's flesh. I hear him scream when the metal spikes dig into his skin. The rest of the men in the room tighten into stiff statues, but they won't interfere or try to stop this on behalf of their friend. The sight of the blood dripping down the man's back is bad, but his screams are worse. His screams reveal how bad the torture really is.

Nacio brings the whip down three times in quick succession, and Karp's screams become deafening. I close my eyes, but it only amplifies his screams.

I open my eyes and look at Kinsley, who is staring at Nacio. She doesn't look away. Instead, she watches intently as the man is whipped. Occasionally, I watch her eyes drift closed when it all becomes too much.

After fifteen lashes, Nacio stops. I glance at the man's back covered in blood. I don't think he will last much longer. I think he will ask for death rather than more lashes. Nacio walks away from him. Karp will only survive if Nacio decides he has had enough lashes.

Nacio stops in front of Kinsley. "Want a try?" he asks, holding the whip up to Kinsley.

I watch Kinsley's eyes widen as she looks at the handle of the whip Nacio is holding out to her. She doesn't react, even though I can see the conflict in her eyes. This could cement her place. Ensure that Nacio trusts her. Karp deserves to be beaten. Every man in this room deserves it. But I'm not sure Kinsley can inflict the justice. She just looks at the whip, almost studying it.

"You are going to have to finish yourself, Nacio. Kinsley doesn't have it in her to beat a man, even a man as guilty as Karp," Lee says.

Kinsley immediately grabs the whip from Nacio's hand. Nacio grins wildly while Granddad frowns. I wonder if her granddad was egging her on because he wants her to join him or because he wants her to prove him right, so he can get rid of her. From the look of disappointment on his face, I would guess it was the latter.

Kinsley walks up to the same place where Nacio was just standing. She turns back to Nacio, and I think she is going to change her mind. She can't beat another man, even a man as horrible and vile as Karp.

She can't do it.

And, if she does, she is going to regret it. So, as much as I know it will help her standing with these men, I don't want her to do it. Whipping *me* was one thing. Whipping *him*, drawing blood from a man who is getting no pleasure from it, is something entirely different.

She looks to Nacio. "How many are left?"

"Fifteen," Nacio says.

Kinsley turns back to the man and brings the whip up just like Nacio did. She brings it down hard and sharp against his skin. Karp screams out again, but it's not as deafening as his previous screams. The whip still struck his skin, but she doesn't have the same finesse or power that Nacio just used.

I watch her chest rise and fall as her adrenaline sinks in. I can see a hint of nerves bubbling under her skin at the thought of having to hit a man fourteen more times while listening to his bloodcurdling screams. She doesn't hesitate for longer than a second though before she brings the whip up and down again. This one is even weaker than the first.

I glance over at Nacio and her granddad. They are staring intently at Kinsley. Nacio has a large grin on his face as he walks over to her and stands behind her.

He holds on to her arm and shows her how to lift the whip. "Like this," he says as he helps her use the whip again.

This time, Karp's scream returns to the bloodcurdling one it was earlier. This scream makes the whole room shake again with terror.

Nacio steps back and watches Kinsley whip Karp again with the same speed and sharpness he just did. Nacio's grin grows larger. He thinks he's won. He thinks she is on his side now.

She isn't. She's mine. All mine.

I want to scream that to him. I want to punch him for touching Kinsley. For forcing her to do this. The only thing that stops me is that I know they would kill me in front of her, and I can't let her experience that pain. A pain I have felt before when I thought she was dead.

Kinsley glances up and I know she's imagining the woman who was raped, and I don't know what she sees, but something changes inside of her. She has renewed strength at what she must do, and this time, she hits Karp with all the power she has. As she does, her face seems content and satisfied.

She moves again, and I watch the satisfaction grow on her face. I watch the pleasure spread through her body as she hits him. I don't know what the pleasure is from. *Is it from inflicting pain on another person?*

I try to close my eyes. I try not to see the pleasure engulfing her body with each whip, but I can't keep my eyes off of her. Because I quickly realize what changed. In order to get through this, she shut out this room, and returned to the room with me in that cell. She's imagining my screams instead of Karp. She's riding my cock pulling my pleasure from me along with the blood.

She stops for a second to remove her jacket, exposing her bare stomach and black lace bra. Now, there is no way I will ever be able to take my eyes off of her again. She looks sexy, standing there, with a whip in her hand, and I suddenly want her fantasies to be true. I wish she were whipping me, not him. Even though the whip in her hand is a million times more painful than the one she used on me, I still want it.

I want to feel the sting of it on my skin as she looks at me with desire.

She whips again, but this time, Karp doesn't scream. I look at him, and I think he has passed out from the pain. She needs to stop. She could kill him.

But she doesn't stop. Kinsley lifts the whip and thrusts it forward again and again.

Each time she does, my cock grows harder and harder. Each time, I want to beg for her to touch me, to whip me. Each time she whips him, I see the desire growing behind her eyes as well. She's back in the room with me, not him.

We're twisted, so fucking twisted. We are both aroused

by her whipping. If she touched me or even looked at me right now, I'd come. And I know she'd be right behind me.

Because at first, she whipped Karp to cement her place here. To further earn Nacio's trust. After seeing the woman Karp raped, she whipped him harder to extract the revenge the woman would never get a chance to extract. But now, she's whipping him because it is bringing her back to that cell with me.

I've brought her into the darkness with me.

I watch her pant with lust and need as she quickly hits him, each time going faster and faster. My breathing picks up, and my heart rate builds to an unbearable pace. My cock twitches and aches for her. I feel like I'm going to burst if I don't come soon. I'm afraid I will die if she doesn't touch me.

She whips again, and this time, she screams an orgasmic, harsh scream I haven't heard from her before. The scream is enough. The pressure that has been building in both of us is suddenly gone. It left when she screamed. It's gone, as simple as that, and it's replaced with Kinsley's anger. I see the rage forming the second the release disappeared. A anger caused by what her family did to countless people. Frustration with me for lying. Anger at Karp for hurting that woman. Everything in her world comes crashing down now that the high she felt is gone.

She becomes wild and lashes the end of the whip toward Karp, but her movements are no longer smooth and practiced. Now, they are wild and untamed.

Nacio walks over to her, barely missing getting hit by the whip himself. He tightly wraps his arms around her. "Enough. He's had enough, baby." He nestles his face in the crevice of her neck.

My face rages with so much anger as I see him touch her

after such an intimate moment. I can feel the steam rolling off my bare skin.

Nacio tucks her hair behind her ear. "You did well, baby."

I watch her breathing slow at his words, and I hate him. I hate him for comforting her. I hate him for calming her anger. I know that, once the anger at Karp is gone, once the anger at her situation completely disappears, a new hate will form. I've felt the hate before when I caused my brother's death. When I thought I had failed Kinsley, I felt the same.

Kinsley will hate herself.

17

KINSLEY

I hate myself.

I should kill myself.

I should pull Nacio's gun out from his waistband and kill myself. I am a horrible person. I can't believe what I just did. I destroyed a man, and I enjoyed it. I'm just like Nacio. Just like Granddad. Just like my father.

I truly am a Felton. A monster.

I'm twisted. I just whipped a man, and I've never been more turned on. Once the whip got in my hand, the images of Killian came floating back. The need to bring the woman justice helped me start. The anger flowed, quickly turning to lust for Killian. But even if the man deserved it, I shouldn't have done it. And I definitely shouldn't have enjoyed one second of it. I deserve to die.

Nacio slowly releases me and looks to his men in the room. "This is what happens when you disobey an order. I don't care who you are or how long you've worked for us. Never disobey," Nacio points to Karp, who I swear must be dead against the pole.

His body is slack, and I don't see his chest moving. He's not breathing. *He's dead.* I killed him. I killed someone. I feel the butterflies I kept hidden forming in my stomach, making me queasy.

Nacio nods at the men. They begin filing out of the room. I don't chance a glance at Killian even though I can feel his eyes on me. I can't bear to look at him and see his disappointment in me.

The room empties, except for Nacio, Granddad, Karp, and me. Nacio, Granddad, and I stare at the man who is still bleeding in the center of the room.

Two men come back into the room.

"Get him down, and clean him up. Get him medical care if he needs it," Nacio says.

The men exchange glances and then walk over to where Karp's body is. *He's dead,* I think, as his body falls to the ground in a limp pile. They cut the rope, keeping his arms attached to the rope.

He's dead. I killed him.

The men reach under his arms, lifting him. Karp groans, proving me wrong. He is still very much alive—at least for now. The men begin dragging him out of the room.

I don't wait. I can't stand to be in here any longer.

I run past them before they get to the door. I need air. That is my only mission. I don't care if it is breaking the rules. I need to get out of here.

My stomach begins churning as soon as I make it out of the room. I won't make it down the stairs and outside before I lose it. I move to the hallway window a foot away from me. I try to push it open, but it doesn't budge. I try the latch, but it is frozen. My stomach churns again, warning me I don't have much time. I glance out the window and see a balcony. It looks to be down the hallway, to my right.

I run as fast as I can, holding my stomach and praying the contents won't come up. I can't let them see how I react. I have to get out of here. I push the door open to what used to be an apartment. I run across what looks to be an old living room to the sliding door of the balcony. I grab the handle to throw it open and am relieved when it creaks and opens enough for my body to fit through.

Breathe.

I finally breathe, and I taste the fresh air from outside. But the air isn't enough to settle my sick stomach. I grab the railing just as the contents of my stomach come up. Thank God the street is empty, and no one is walking below me.

"Here," Nacio suddenly says from behind me.

I come up for another breath between vomits.

I feel his hand on my back in a surprisingly comforting manner I didn't expect from him.

I turn to face him and see him holding a glass of water in his hand.

"Thanks," I say, taking the glass from him. I sip on the water, and it immediately relaxes my stomach.

Nacio's hand stays on my back, slowly moving in calming circles. Although this man became the monster that he is, I know there is something better inside him. He has kept some part of him buried for far too long. Maybe, if I can appeal to that part of him, he can help me put an end to all of this. I just need to find that small part of him again.

"You did amazing back there, baby. I'm proud of you."

I shake my head. "And then I puked. I'm not sure I'll ever be cut out for this job."

He laughs. "Sure you will. It just takes some time to get used to the blood, to the smell. We've all puked before. It doesn't take away from what you did back there."

I nod.

"How do you feel?"

"Queasy and guilty that I enjoyed torturing another man."

Nacio's grin widens. "That's what makes you cut out for this job. Nobody enjoys it if they aren't cut out for this."

I try to force a smile onto my own lips, but it's hard. I don't want to be cut out for this. I don't want to be tempted into this world. I want to put a stop to this.

"Does that mean I passed?"

"Yes, but you still need to kill the FBI agent. After that, you will have full access to everything."

"Have we heard anything about the FBI in Mexico?"

He moistens his lips as he tucks a loose strand of my hair behind my ear. "So impatient, baby. Don't worry. You will get to kill him soon. We haven't heard yet if the FBI has found our place in Mexico, but they will soon."

I nod.

"Come on." He holds his hand out to me. "I want to show you something."

I place my hand in his, despite my gut telling me not to.

We walk back inside. We walk past the room where I beat a man almost to death. I try not to look inside as we pass. I pray I don't run into Granddad or Mother. I pray we don't run into anyone as we make our way back downstairs.

We don't.

Nacio walks outside, still holding my hand, and that's when I realize I'm wearing a bra and jeans on the streets of Paris. Nacio notices my free arm curl around my stomach.

He pulls me to him in an awkward hold. "Stop. You're beautiful."

I smile, but I hate his words. I hate that a tiny butterfly returns to my stomach when he looks at me. I hate that I am even a little bit attracted to a man who isn't Killian. I hate that I'm affected at all. I hate that I get the tiniest tingling for a man whom I watched kill an innocent woman.

As soon as the image of the woman comes back into my head, the tingling disappears. The butterfly in my stomach disappears. I gently pull out of his arms, not able to stand being in them.

"Where are we going?"

"My house," he says, frowning at me as I stand two feet away from him instead of in his arms. "It's fifteen blocks from here. You able to walk that far?"

I nod.

He holds his hand back out, and I place my hand back in his, despite the urge I have to keep my hands firmly wrapped around my midriff.

We walk in silence down the beautiful streets of Paris. We pass other couples who are holding hands, and they smile at us with knowing looks on their faces. They think we are together. They think we are lovers, but that is something we could never be.

We turn the corner, and I begin to feel the pain as I walk in my black heels. My feet are sore with blisters I'm not used to experiencing, ones that shouldn't be there after such a short walk. I pause for a second to try to fix the heels, so they stop rubbing against my blisters.

Nacio pauses with me and then steps in front of me. "Climb on." He bends down a little, giving me his back.

I hesitate. I don't want to climb onto his back, not unless I get to slit his throat when I do. I climb onto his back anyway because I know I won't make it if I have to walk any farther. I don't understand why we are walking at all, other than Nacio wanting an excuse for me to climb onto his back.

Nacio stands back up, tightly holding on to my legs,

while I reluctantly hold on to his neck. I can't help but breathe in his scent as we walk. The smell of his cologne makes me close my eyes as it reminds me of Killian. It's not quite the same scent, but it's close enough to bring me back to him. I remember he is locked up in a cell somewhere in severe pain while I complain about my feet hurting. I really am a spoiled princess.

Nacio walks several more blocks before we turn another corner.

"This is your house?"

He sighs, relaxing at the sight of his palace he calls his Paris home. A gate stands between us and his house, blocking some of the house, but I can tell from here his house is at least three times the size of ours in Las Vegas.

"How were you able to afford something so grand? My family's house in Las Vegas isn't even this large."

"I inherited it from my father," he says somberly.

I slide down his back, willing to walk the rest of the way to his house. We pause at the gate, and he enters a code. And then we take the quarter of a mile walk up the entrance gardens full of green trees and vines with just a few pops of color from the flowers. I don't understand how a monster lives here.

We walk up to the door, and he unlocks it with a key he pulled from his pocket. I expect to immediately be greeted by staff members welcoming Nacio home, but I don't see anyone rushing to us.

"Is anyone here?"

Nacio glances down at me, and his eyes widen. "You seriously think I would have staff here?"

I shrug. "Yes. Who cooks and cleans for you? Who does your laundry? Who takes care of the gardens?"

"Me."

Now, it's my turn to raise my eyebrows. "Really?"

"Yes. I don't like having other people cook or clean. I have two security guards, but that's it. I like my privacy."

I nod. I glance up, looking at the beautiful chandelier hanging overhead. I could stay here forever, just looking at it, but Nacio grabs my hand and pulls me through the foyer to a large room at the back. This room is a large dining hall with a ceiling at least two stories tall.

"Sit," he says, pointing to a chair at a long dark table that could easily seat twenty.

"You don't want to show me around the rest of the place?"

"No, you need to eat first."

On cue, my stomach growls, giving me away.

"Fair enough, but don't you need time to cook?" I grab my stomach that still feels a little queasy after being sick earlier.

"No, I'll have to cook for you another time."

Nacio walks through the door of the dining hall to what I assume is the kitchen. He returns a second later with glasses, a wine bottle, and a plate of cheese.

He places each on the table and then begins pouring us each a glass of wine. He then pulls matches out of his pocket and lights the candles nearest to us even though it's not dark out yet. I watch as he takes a seat on the end, kitty-corner to me.

He lifts his glass of red wine, and I do the same.

"To us," he says, clinking his glass against mine.

I take a sip but then immediately regret it. This wine isn't sweet. It's harsh and bitter. I won't be able to do more than sip it. It's nothing like the wine Killian has gotten for me.

I grab one of the squares of cheese on the tray in the

center of the table and pop it into my mouth. This, on the other hand, tastes like heaven. I grab a handful of the cheese and continue popping several into my mouth until my stomach begins to settle a little.

"How did your father die?"

"He didn't die," Nacio says, frowning at me.

"Oh..." I pause between bites of cheese. "I thought you said you inherited this place from your father."

"I did, but he didn't die. He is running our location in Asia."

Fuck. There is another location. Another place for pain and suffering.

"Oh, where in Asia?" I ask casually before popping another piece of cheese into my mouth.

Nacio takes a bite of cheese himself. "I inherited this house and this location when my father chose to move to Asia. We will have to travel there at some point. I haven't visited that location yet. We have spent most of our time traveling between Mexico and Paris. But this location is my favorite. Santino prefers the darkness of Mexico. I prefer the light of Paris. My father prefers the excitement of Asia."

"What about my family? What did my father prefer? My grandfather?"

He thinks for a second. "Your grandfather prefers Mexico. It was hard for him to give up that location. Although we will start up a new location in South America soon. And your father, Paris. I think that's why he and I got along so well. It killed me to see him die."

"You were there when he died?"

Nacio nods.

"You were in Las Vegas?" I sit up straighter in my seat.

He nods again. "I was there when your father died."

"So, it really wasn't a heart attack?"

"It wasn't a heart attack. Killian killed him. He poisoned your father and made it look like a heart attack."

I feel a tear fall down my face. I know that Nacio isn't speaking the truth. I know that Killian didn't kill my father. But I still don't understand who did, and I might never know. Even though I hate him, I still care for him deep down, which kills me. It kills me that I'm crying for my father when he was a monster. Maybe, now that I am one, too, I feel more for him than I should. I feel connected to him.

I glance to Nacio, who wipes the tear from my cheek. There's a softness, a kindness, in Nacio, just like my father. I didn't have the opportunity to turn my father from the darkness, but I can bring Nacio to my side. I just don't have any idea how to do that, other than to flirt and let him flirt back.

"I miss him," I say.

"Me, too."

Nacio tucks a strand of hair behind my ear, and I grab his hand, keeping it pressed against my cheek. I close my eyes, trying to imagine his hand is Killian's, but that won't work. Nacio is nothing like Killian. Nacio is selfish, ruthless, and intimidating. Killian is loving, selfless, and intense. Their strength and ability to lie to me might be the only similarities between the two men.

I open my eyes, no longer able to fantasize that Nacio is Killian. I place my hand on the nape of Nacio's neck and pull him to me until his lips are pressed against mine. He aggressively kisses me. His tongue thrusts in and out of my mouth, making it hard for me to breathe. I continue to hold on to his neck, trying to hold on to dear life, as he grabs my other hand and pulls it hard to his chest. Harder than what

I'm comfortable with. A painful moan escapes my lips when he pulls my hair with his other hand. I try to make it sound sexy, but there is no mistaking my moan for anything other than pain.

I pull at his hair and hear his painful growl in return. Fuck, I don't know how to stop this. He must hear my thoughts though because he aggressively releases me. He wipes his mouth with the back of his hand. We both breathe hard and fast, trying to catch our breaths after a kiss like that.

He has a wicked, dirty grin plastered on his face as he looks at me, and I'm afraid I've ignited his lust for me. I'm afraid he is going to want to fuck me right this second, but I can't let him.

"You and I would make quite a pair. I don't trust you yet, not fully. But I will soon, and then we can take over everything together."

"How?" I ask when my breathing has returned.

"We will kill them. *All of them.*"

My mouth drops a little at his suggestion, but maybe I misunderstood him.

"What do you mean, kill all of them? Who exactly?"

"Your grandfather, your mother, my brother, and my father. We kill them all, and then we will be free. We kill all of them, and then we can do what we want with the organization."

His face brightens. This isn't the first time he has thought about this. I can tell from his excitement. This is what he really wants. I just don't understand why.

I sip on the bitter wine, trying to mask my disgust at what he is suggesting. I set the glass back down. "You could really do that? You could kill your father? Your brother?"

"Yes," he answers automatically.

I know he is telling me the truth. He's not lying.

"Could you? Could you kill your grandfather and mother?"

I don't have to think about it. I already know my answer. "Yes."

18

KILLIAN

I'VE BEEN in this dark room for hours. My stomach growls, letting me know how hungry I am, as if the ache isn't enough to let me know. My body is sore from being tied up, from lack of sleep, and from not eating in days. If they don't plan on putting a bullet in my head soon, I will easily die from lack of food and water.

At least, this time, I can move around. My arms are still tied behind my back, but they didn't tie me to anything. So, I could move around if only I found the strength to move from my position on the floor.

I glance around the small room I'm sure used to be a closet. The door looks weak, compared to the door that was keeping me in when we were in Mexico. I could try to kick it in. But then what? I would have to run, but I'm not sure I have the strength to do that, not without getting caught. If they caught me, there would be a good chance they would shoot me on the spot.

I try to sit up, but just lifting my head is painful and exhausting. So, I don't bother again. I just need to rest. Once I rest, I will have enough strength to form a good plan.

I close my eyes and think of Kinsley. I try to let her stay in my thoughts. But the darkness soon overtakes me.

"We can kill him soon," Seth says.

I open my eyes, expecting to see Seth standing in front of me, but he's not. The darkness is still covering me. He must be just outside my door though. That confirms that, even if I kicked the door down, I wouldn't be able to escape with Seth just outside the door.

"Good, I don't like keeping him alive," Lee says.

"The FBI has found our location in Mexico. It's all over the news. They seem to think they have found everyone who was behind your deaths," Seth says.

"Good. We just need to verify that before we kill him. I expect he will be dead by tomorrow," Lee says.

"What about Kinsley, Nacio, and Santino? They could ruin everything. What are we going to do about them?" Seth says.

"Santino isn't a threat. He will do whatever we say. And, as for Kinsley and Nacio..." Lee says.

My eyes grow heavier as they speak until I'm barely able to keep my eyes open. Until I can barely hear the words they are saying.

"We can handle them, just like..."

19

KINSLEY

I'M SITTING in Granddad's office with Mother, Nacio, and Santino. They are discussing what prices they are getting for the five children we just got in and where they will be going. The prices are insane, all in the millions, and they are throwing the numbers around like it is nothing.

What's worse is the way they talk about the children. As if they aren't children. Just objects to be bought, sold, and rented.

"So, it's agreed. Nacio and Santino will take the shipment to London," Granddad says.

"What about Killian?" Santino asks.

"We will take him with us. We can kill him and throw him over the yacht. He won't ever be found," Nacio says.

Everyone nods in agreement.

"Kinsley can come with us and do the honors," Nacio says.

"I'd love to," I say.

Nacio winks at me. After our last conversation, he thinks I'm on his side. He thinks I will do whatever he says, and I will. I will because getting close to Nacio might be my only chance at keeping Killian alive.

I watch as the five kids—two boys and three girls—are escorted from the bus to a private yacht. I watch them walk what could be their last walk where they are completely unharmed. They haven't been raped or tortured or murdered. This could be the last time they experience even a shred of happiness even if it is only from the warm sun beating down on us.

I can't let them get hurt. I can't let them be sold. I can't.

I watch the three men escorting them. They are so unfazed by what they are doing. Santino is escorting the first two, followed by two men I don't recognize. All of them seem calm and relaxed, like they are just going for an afternoon walk, not walking children to their deaths. I don't know what to do, but I know I can't let it happen. *I won't.*

Next off the bus are Killian and Nacio. Killian doesn't try to hide his stares this time. This time, he locks his gaze on me as he walks past where I'm standing on the base of the ramp of the yacht. I glance to Nacio, who is also staring at me. Both men are showing me how much they want me. Both men are devouring me with their eyes, and I can't give either of them the reaction they want.

I wait for them to walk past me, and then I follow them onto the large yacht that could easily fit twenty-plus people. I watch as the men take the children down the stairs inside the yacht. Nacio follows with Killian while I stay on the deck of the yacht. I can't stand to go downstairs with them. I wouldn't be able to keep my composure. I couldn't keep from trying to kill all of the men who are walking so calmly down the stairs.

I walk over to the edge and look out at the water that is so calm and beautiful. The sun is setting over the water. It's beautiful here. Riding on a yacht like this in such a luxurious setting should be beautiful, but all I can think about is that this might be the last beautiful thing I see as well because we might all be dead by morning.

"It's beautiful, just like you," Nacio says from behind me.

He wraps his arms around me, like a lover would do, except he is a monster and I'm far from a lover. Still, we stay like this for a while as the yacht begins moving away from the dock. I feel weirdly calm with his arms wrapped around me. Nacio has a weird way of making me feel like he's a good person who cares about me one second, and then the next second, he's the devil who wants to destroy people's lives. I can't understand him.

"We are going to play cards. You want to play?" one of the men asks from behind us.

Nacio looks to me.

"Sure," I say.

I follow the man down the stairs. A large kitchen, complete with marble countertops, sits at the bottom of the stairs with three tables. Past that seems to be a lounge area. A man is sitting at the first table with a deck of cards, tequila, and chips and salsa spread out on the table. I smile at the man, but he doesn't smile back at me as I sit down next to him at the table.

Nacio sits next to me, followed by the man who invited us down to play.

"Where's Santino?" I ask.

"Driving the boat," Nacio answers.

"And who is watching..." I can't finish the sentence. I

can't say *kids* or *prisoners* or *shipment*, as they often call them. I can't say any of those words.

"No one. There is no need. We are in the middle of the ocean, and they are locked up. We don't have to worry about them until morning," Nacio says.

I nod.

"I'm Kinsley," I say to the two men whom I haven't met before. "What are we playing?"

"I'm Don," the younger man across from me says. He looks to be close to my age, and he has blond hair and green eyes. He doesn't have the monster look yet.

I glance to the other man who looks slightly older, probably because of his eyes. His glare makes him look more menacing than Don. His hair is darker, and his stubble is thicker than Don's.

"Maurice," he says somberly.

"Poker. That's all the men know how to play. You know how to play poker?" Nacio asks.

"Yes. I know the basics. What are we playing for?"

"We usually play for duties, but since you both are the bosses, I don't think that is the best idea," Don says.

We all nod.

"Strip poker?" Nacio suggests.

I roll my eyes. That isn't going to happen.

I glance around the room, trying to come up with something we could play for, but all I see are the tequila and tortilla chips. Tequila—that's my only hope. If I can win enough games and get them drunk enough, I might have hope at getting the kids safely off the boat. I might have a chance at saving Killian.

"How about shots? Everyone that loses each round has to take a tequila shot. And when you lose all of your poker chips, you have to take three."

The men shrug. I stand and pull four shot glasses out of the cabinet while the men pass out poker chips from a case beneath the table.

I watch as Maurice begins dealing out cards. I get a two and a seven. The men begin betting, only speaking to place their bets. I call and then watch the flop. None of the cards on the table go with the cards in my hand.

I am forced to fold, which causes me to have to take a shot. Don pours me a shot of tequila, and I down the glass. It burns down my throat. Nacio wins the hand and forces Don and Maurice to take a shot as well.

This isn't going to work unless I win a majority of the games. I need them to pass out from the drinks, but if I pass out first, I won't be able to save anyone.

Don deals the next round.

I lose. I drink.

After the third hand, I've had three shots while everyone else has split shots evenly among themselves.

I deal the fourth hand and finally win. I relax a little. But poker is a game of chance, especially with how the game is set up. The only way to keep from drinking is to win every hand, which is hard to do.

So, on my next deal, I make sure to make my own luck. I hide a pair of kings I'll use the next time I think I will lose a hand. It causes me to win three in a row, so all of the men have to drink. My head is spinning from the three shots I have had while most of the men at the table have had close to eight. Their heads must be pounding.

"I should go check on Santino," Nacio says after another loss.

I glance at his pile of chips. "Not until I've won."

He smiles. "Or I could just give you all of my chips now."

"No. I want to win fair and square."

"You've been cheating," Maurice says next to me.

I freeze. "Have not."

He smiles for the first time all night. "Relax. There is no way a pretty girl like you could cheat."

He slurs his words, and I know he's getting close to blacking out from the alcohol. So, instead of playing another hand, I grab the bottle of tequila that is almost empty, and I pour everyone a shot.

I lift my shot glass. "To Nacio, for the kick-ass yacht."

Nacio tries to smile at me but only one side of his lips curls up. "To you."

We clink glasses together, sloppily spilling half of our shots, before knocking them back.

I stand from the table and stumble as I get up. I've had more to drink than I planned on.

"You okay?" Nacio asks.

I nod and then sloppily kiss Nacio on the cheek. "Bathroom. Be right back to finish kicking your asses."

I stumble through the kitchen to the bathroom just before the base of the stairs. I take my time in the bathroom, hoping to God my plan works. I can't shoot Killian, and I won't ever be able to live with myself if I let those kids go. I wait almost twenty minutes and then decide I've waited long enough.

I slowly emerge from the bathroom and tiptoe to where the men are sitting. Maurice is snoring loudly. Don has moved from the table to the couch. His eyes are closed, and he seems to be asleep. Nacio has his head resting on the table, his breathing slow and easy.

I sigh and tuck a loose strand of hair behind my ear. They are asleep. I just don't know for how long or how deep of a sleep they are in. I slowly back out of the kitchen until I find the stairs at the back of the yacht. I pause at the stairs and glance back to where the men are sitting to see if any of them have moved. They haven't, so I take my chance.

I move as quietly but as quickly as I can down the stairs, knowing my time is limited, but I have to take this chance. It might be the only chance I will ever get. By the time I make it down the stairs, my head spins from the tequila, so much so that I can barely walk in a straight line. But I keep moving forward, regardless that it isn't in a straight line.

I get to the first door. I turn the knob and push it open. I find an empty bedroom. No Killian. No kids.

I leave the door open and move to the second door, hoping I find them soon. Every second I don't is another chance I take that one of the men could wake up. The second room is empty, too.

I glance down the hallway and count ten other doors. I don't have time for this.

"Killian," I whisper as I now run down the hallway, pushing every door open but not finding him.

I get to the last two doors. I try to push the second to last door open, but it doesn't open. The knob doesn't turn.

"Killian," I whisper again.

I wait a second.

"Kinsley?" Killian whispers back.

I sigh in relief from just knowing that I've found him.

"I need to get you out, but the door is locked. Can you unlock it from the inside?"

A second passes and then another as I wait for Killian to answer me.

"No, I can't open it. What are you doing here?"

"Getting you out. I don't have time to explain. We don't have much time, and we have to be quiet."

"You're going to have to find a way to unlock it from out

there. I'm tied up, and even if I weren't, the door can't be unlocked from the inside."

"Do you know who would have the key?" I ask.

"No."

I think for a moment, trying to decide on what to do. I could try to search the men for the key, but that would be risky. They could wake up. I could pick the lock, but I have no idea how to do that or even if I could find the tools. I could kick down the door, but it would be loud, and I would risk waking them up, or Santino could hear us from where he is driving the yacht.

"Can we pick the lock?" I ask.

"Have you ever done that before?"

"No."

"Okay. I can try to walk you through it. Do you have a hairpin?"

"No," I sigh. I think back to all the bedrooms. If a woman or girl stayed in any of them, there is a good chance one fell on the floor. "Hold on though." I run through bedroom after bedroom, searching the bathrooms and floors to find a hairpin. I get lucky in the third room, finding a hairpin lying in the corner of the bathroom floor.

I run back to the room where Killian is locked inside. "I have a hairpin."

"Good. You need to break it in half."

I easily break it. "Okay, it's broken."

"One half, you need to bend, so it is curved like a hook," he says, his voice so calm.

My hands are shaking viciously. "Done."

"The other half, you need to bend the end just a little."

I bend it, but I must bend it too far because it breaks.

"It broke," I say in a panicked voice.

If I can't get him out, he's going to die.

"It's okay. Just try again." His voice stays calm.

I bend it slower this time, and it doesn't break. "Okay. Now what?"

"Put the hooked one in the bottom and the slightly bent one on top."

I do it.

"Then, slowly move the top one in to lift each barrel, keeping pressure on the bottom one. You have to lift each lever to get it to unlock."

I begin thinking this is never going to happen, that I'm never going to figure it out, but it unlocks easily with hardly any effort. I push the door open and see Killian standing on the other side of the door. His hands are tied firmly behind his back.

Tears streak down my face at the sight of him. I run over and throw my arms around him, and my lips go to his. Even though his hands are tied behind his back, he still sucks me in and holds me with his body, with his lips. It's a feeling I never thought I would get again. Every emotion I have been holding in every time I am around him comes flooding back as his lips kiss mine. Love, hunger, need. My desire overtakes my body and thoughts with each kiss. With each kiss, I forget more and more of why we are here. That we are in danger. That we have to stop.

All I can think about is my need for him. I need him filling me. I need him to keep devouring me like this. I need...

I hear a scream from the room next to us as the yacht rocks harder when we hit a rough patch. We are out of time.

"We have to go," I say as I force my lips off of Killian's.

Killian turns. "Untie me."

I try to untie him, but I can't. "There's a knife upstairs. I can use it to cut the rope off."

He nods. "Go. I'll start working on talking to the kids."

I run down the hallway, back to the stairs. I slow as I move my way up, trying to keep my steps quiet. When I get to the top, another wave hits just as I reach the door. I grab the handle to keep from falling over and to keep from squealing. The kids downstairs don't hold back though. I can hear their squeals from here.

I slowly walk to the kitchen, being as quiet as I can be, as I pull a knife from a drawer. The whole time, I keep my eyes glued on the men in the room, hoping they will stay asleep. Another wave hits, and I swear, Nacio opens one of his eyes. I freeze, trying to come up with a reason I would be holding a knife. But I can't come up with one. He doesn't move though, and when I look again, his eyes are closed. I must have imagined it.

I quickly run back downstairs to Killian, who is trying to calm the kids at the door.

"We are going to get you out, but you have to be quiet," Killian says through the door.

He sees me, and I know he isn't as sure they are going to get out. I walk behind him and immediately start working on cutting the ropes holding his hands together.

"They are still asleep upstairs, but I don't know for how much longer."

"There is a small boat on the back. We can all fit on it. We will head straight for the shore. It's a long shot because this yacht could easily outrun the smaller lifeboat, but it's our only shot."

"I agree. I'll try to stall them for as long as I can to give you a chance."

The ropes come undone just as Killian turns to me with intensity in his eyes. "You're coming with us." He firmly grabs my hands, and I know he will drag me on the boat if I don't convince him.

"I can't."

"Why the hell not?"

"Because there are more locations than just Paris. There is one in Asia."

"Where in Asia?"

"I don't know, but if I can earn Nacio's trust, he might tell me. And I need to make sure that when the FBI comes, they find them. That they don't run. The FBI will need someone on the inside."

Killian runs his hand through his hair. "I don't like it. I should be the one who stays, not you."

I shake my head. "They will kill you if you stay."

He raises his eyebrow at me. "And they won't kill you?"

"No, they won't. They have no reason to believe I helped you. Why would I help you and then stay? It doesn't make sense."

"Exactly, it makes no sense. I'm not leaving you."

20

———

KILLIAN

Kinsley helps the last kid onto the boat.

"Get on. I'll give the boat a good push to get us going so we won't have to start the engine until we are far enough away we won't be heard," I say.

Kinsley nods as she steps on and begins untying the rope. She fought me, but I convinced her it wasn't safe for her here. That she has to come with. We will contact the FBI immediately. They will get here in time to save the women and find the other facility in Asia.

When the rope is loose, I push the boat as hard as I can and jump on, knowing my weight will propel the boat forward.

I exhale. We aren't safe, not yet, but we are together. And as close to safety as we've been.

I turn with a small smile to keep the kids calm, and then I move to Kinsley.

Fuck.

I turn completely around when I find the empty seat where Kinsley was supposed to be sitting.

Kinsley is standing on the yacht, staring at me stoically. With love in her eyes she mouths, "I love you."

Fuck, fuck, fuck.

I consider trying to turn around to go back for her, but that would require starting the engine. It would involve risking the lives of the five innocent children on this boat with me.

"I love you too," I mouth back, knowing I can't turn around.

Kinsley smiles at my words. She didn't give me a goodbye kiss, she gave me no warning she was going to stay. She's the strongest woman I know, and though I will worry for her safety, I have no doubt she will fight with everything she has to save every one of those women and children her family and Nacio has hurt.

"I will come back for you," I mouth.

She nods and then turns and disappears back into the boat.

When we are far enough away not to be heard, I start the engine, knowing I'm leaving the love of my life behind. And if anything happens, I won't survive without her. It's the hardest thing I've ever done.

We speed through the water most of the night. I try not to look back, but it is hard not to. It is hard not to think about Kinsley. That I left her to possibly be killed by Nacio as soon as he finds out we are gone. My only hope is that Kinsley is right. That she has Nacio tied around her finger and she can find the last location, so this never happens again.

I glance up at the sky beginning to light, and I know we are about out of time. The yacht was supposed to reach shore by seven in the morning, just an hour or so after sunrise. We need to reach the shore first. We need to get to the police first before they get to us.

I crank the engine, trying to get the boat to go faster, but it doesn't go any faster. I look over at the children who have somehow fallen asleep on each other, despite our situation. It's better this way. It's better if they sleep. Earlier, one of the girls, I think her name was Jill, puked off the side of the boat from seasickness. That caused all but one of the others to puke as well.

I spent the first hour after that trying to distract them, and I learned about all of them. I know all of their names— Jill, Stephanie, Brooke, David, and Jose. I know where all of them are from and how many siblings they each have. I tried to find out as much about them as possible, to distract not only them, but me. To keep me moving forward instead of considering turning back and risking all of their lives.

After an hour though, they all fell asleep, giving me too much time to think about Kinsley. About how it would feel if she died.

I look up when I spot the shore.

"Kids, wake up. We are almost there."

We are going to make it.

And, as soon as I get to shore, I'm going to call the FBI to have them move in as soon as possible to get Kinsley out of there.

Just hold on, Kinsley. Hold on.

21

KINSLEY

"WAKE UP, beautiful. We are almost there," Nacio says while gently shaking my shoulder.

I stir and am greeted with the worst headache possible and a crick in my neck from sleeping on the poker table. I grab my neck as I look up at Nacio. "I need—"

"Here's some Advil and coffee." Nacio hands me the coffee and pills.

"Thanks," I say, taking them from him. "I think we drank too much last night, but I don't remember."

Nacio smiles at me. "You'll feel better soon. We won't drink as much on the way back."

"Good." I sip the coffee, hoping it will cure my headache.

After Killian left, I came back and knocked back a couple more shots, so I could pretend I passed out, just like the rest of them. And also to get the image of Killian out of my head. I know I did the right thing forcing him to leave with the children, but the look on his face. The worry around his eyes and pain at being forced into leaving me here was an image I will never forget. I regret drinking so much now.

"Go check on them downstairs, and get them ready to be moved," Nacio says to Maurice and Don.

I try to remain calm, knowing they are going to find the bedrooms empty. But my heart flutters so loudly I'm afraid Nacio can hear me.

"Have you ever been to London?" Nacio asks me.

"Yes. A couple of times with my father."

Nacio nods. "I want to take you to one restaurant on the river before we head back tonight."

"Sounds wonderful."

"Um...sir?" Don says nervously at the door.

Nacio angrily glances up. "What is it?" he snaps.

"They're, uh..." He tries to get the words out, but he can't.

"They're gone," Maurice says, stepping up.

Nacio slowly stands from the chair next to me. "What do you mean, they're gone? Where could they have gone?"

"They took the boat off the back. The FBI agent must have helped them."

"Fuck! I knew we should have killed him in Mexico." He glares at me.

I glare back. "I'm sorry. You were right. I thought—"

He slaps me hard on the face. I grab my face. It stings where his hand touched me.

"If I find out you had anything to do with this, I will kill you myself," Nacio says to me.

I glare at him. "I didn't have anything to do with it. I was passed out from the alcohol, same as you. Maybe you should have made sure they couldn't escape. Obviously, one of you fucked up and didn't lock the door. It's the only way they could have escaped."

Maurice and Don turn to Nacio. It's obvious he was the one who locked the door. When he realizes he might have been the one who fucked up, he pauses for just a second.

Then, he starts yelling, "Search the boat, just to be sure, Don! Now!" He turns to Maurice. "Tell Santino to step on it, and keep an eye out for their boat."

He turns to me as he pulls out his phone. "I have to make a call. Help Don search the boat."

I nod and begin walking around the boat. I search downstairs in every bedroom even though I know they aren't here. I search the main deck and upstairs. I check in with Don to see if he has found any clues as to where they went, but he hasn't. When there is nowhere for either of us to look, we go in search of Nacio. We find him with Santino, who is steering the yacht.

"We didn't find anything," Don says.

Nacio turns to us as Santino turns the yacht around.

"They were spotted heading into a police station," Nacio says, his face bright red with anger. He paces back and forth in the small room.

"Are we going to go after them?" I ask.

Nacio stops and looks at me. "No."

Inside, my heart relaxes a little, as I know Killian is safe. He's actually safe, and we aren't going to go after him. We aren't going to bring him back. I can finally relax and let my heart go with him. It's the only way to protect what's left of it.

"So, we are heading back to Paris?"

"Yes. We are heading back, but we can't stay in Paris long. Just long enough to move everyone and destroy any evidence linking us to the other location. We will have to move to our Asia location or go into hiding for a while now that the FBI knows of the Paris location because of Killian."

I swallow down a gulp, seeing his anger because we can't stay at the Paris location. At his favorite location. Because of Killian and me.

"I'm sorry."

He walks to me. "You should be. It's your fault Killian is still alive. It's your fault we have to give up the Paris location. It's your fault we just lost over five million dollars in one day. Lee isn't going to be happy when we get back. And I'm not going to stand up for you. He can do what he wants with you."

Nacio turns back to Santino, and they begin talking about the best course to take back to Paris, effectively ignoring me. I look at Don, who is looking out at the water, ignoring me. I walk back inside to the living room alone.

It's going to be a long day of traveling back to Paris. Nacio might believe I didn't help them escape last night, but he still blames me for keeping Killian alive. And I know Granddad will agree with him. I don't know if Granddad will actually have me killed for that, but whatever he decides, it won't be good.

I just hope the FBI moves in before they have a chance to punish me. I hope the FBI moves in before they have a chance to scatter and hide. But, most of all, I feel like I can breathe for the first time since Killian arrived. Now, Killian is safe, and my heart is free.

22

KILLIAN

I CALLED THE FBI. They will arrive in the morning. I didn't think that was good enough. I wanted them to move in immediately, but they said they needed time to get their agents in location and to ensure all of the criminals were actually at the Paris location before they moved in. That means Kinsley is on her own for one more night.

It's already been an entire day since I left her. An entire day since I ripped out my heart and left it with her. That is why I couldn't go one more night without seeing her and making sure she was still breathing. So, the second I got off the phone with the FBI in London, I was on the next flight to Paris. I've been hiding out in the building across from the Marlows' and Feltons' organization in Paris for hours now, waiting for them to return. Waiting for the FBI to get here in the morning. Waiting to see if Kinsley is still alive.

Just waiting.

I'm tired of fucking waiting.

But I don't have a choice. So, I sit and wait. And pace and wait. And curse and wait.

Darkness begins to fall over the city, and I'm afraid they

decided not to come back to Paris. I'm afraid they decided to move to their Asia location or went into hiding now that they know the FBI and police are on to them.

I consider calling the FBI again and seeing if they tracked them elsewhere when I see a van pull up. I watch as Nacio, Santino, two men I don't know, and Kinsley step out of the van.

I exhale when I see Kinsley. She's still alive.

I watch them walk into the old apartment building, hidden by the cover of darkness.

I text one of the local FBI agents, saying I think they are all here. They text back they need five hours still and to stay where I am and text them if there is a change.

Fuck.

I can't stay.

I'm done waiting.

I don't have a plan. In fact, I have no idea what I'm doing at all as I walk down the stairs of the building that sits across from the one where Kinsley is. I just know I have to be closer to her. I know I have to keep her safe.

I walk out the side of the building into the darkness. I'm not worried about being spotted outside since the street is so dark. I'm worried about the cameras inside the building. The only way to go undetected is to cut the power. But, if I cut the power to just their building, then they might think the FBI is already here.

So, I take my phone out of my pocket and dial Hayes. He owes me one after he had me arrested and put Kinsley at risk.

"Killian, what's wrong? Have they already moved?"

"No, but I need you to turn the power off in the south part of the city."

"Why?"

"Just do it, Hayes. You owe me."

He sighs.

"Hayes?"

"Give me five."

I end the call and wait. Almost exactly five minutes later, the city plunges into darkness, and I take my chance. I cross the street to the building where Kinsley is inside. I walk to the side door, hoping I won't be spotted. I slowly open the door and slip inside.

Complete darkness is all I see once I'm inside the building. I feel around the walls and realize I'm in somebody's office. I move as silently as possible to the door and press my head against it. I hear people moving and yelling on the other side of the door, as they are trying to figure out what to do now that they have no electricity.

I hear Nacio yell at Kinsley and then nothing. I slowly open the door as Nacio begins yelling again, hoping the darkness will hide me. Nacio stops yelling and walks away. I know Kinsley must be here somewhere, but I can't see where she is. I take a chance anyway.

"Kinsley," I whisper.

"Killian?"

I hear her voice coming from my right, so I reach out in that direction. I feel her shoulder. I grab ahold of her arm and pull her toward me and into the office. I quietly close the door behind us.

Her arms engulf me, and I tightly squeeze her. I wasn't sure I was going to get to experience this again. I feel her body relax in my arms the longer I hold her.

"You shouldn't be here, but I'm so glad you are," she whispers.

"There is nowhere else I would be. Even the possibility of death couldn't keep me away."

She reaches up and grabs my cheeks, pulling me down toward her so she can firmly kiss me on the lips. A kiss we were denied when she decided to stay on the yacht instead of coming with me. Her tongue slips inside my mouth, and I tangle my hand in her hair and listen to her beautiful soft moans as I deepen the kiss.

"I've missed you, princess."

She moans again before pulling my lips back to hers. I try to let myself get lost in the kiss. It would be easy to just let go. Kinsley makes it easy for me to let go. I can't let go though. She's not safe, and I have to protect her.

I grab her shoulders and pull her lips from mine. "We need to go."

She takes a step back. "No, I can't leave. Not yet, not until they are all in FBI custody."

"You have to leave with me. The FBI will be here in five hours."

"By then, they could already be gone."

"Please, princess. You've done your job. Let the FBI do theirs."

"No. I need to be getting back. I'm supposed to be helping pack things up for our trip to Tokyo."

"Do you think that is where their other base of operation is?"

"I don't know, but I plan to find out. Nacio is talking to the city to try to get the electricity back. I guess we can't get into one of our vaults where they keep the money without electricity. As soon as we get electricity back, I'm supposed to meet downstairs to help transfer the money to the vans."

I lift her chin and kiss her hard on the lips. I'm hoping, if I tempt her, she will decide to come back with me instead of staying here. I feel her try to pull away from me, but I don't let her. I won't let her risk herself again. Instead, I walk us backward in the room that has been converted into an office. I kiss her, trying to make her forget about what she is here to do. She moans softly, but I know it's not enough for her to forget what she is doing here.

I feel the door I came in from behind me as I move my lips to her neck. I feel her purring against my lips. I need to make her moan. I need to make her scream, and she can't do that in here.

I grab the door handle, and I pull her outside.

"What"—she pants—"are"—she sucks in as my lips touch her neck again—"you"—she exhales deeply—"doing?"

I grin against her neck. "Making you change your mind."

She moans and grabs my head, forcing my lips on hers. Her tongue is on my tongue. My cock is pressed against her stomach.

"I don't think that's possible. I've already made up my mind."

I reach my hand under her bra and run my thumb over her hard nipple. I watch as her body convulses with just the touch. "I've made you change your mind before," I say into her ear as I squeeze her nipple again, making her pant.

She reaches into my jeans and grabs ahold of my cock that is already hard for her. "I need you now. It can't wait."

She slowly moves her hand up and down my thick cock. I grow harder, willing to give her anything she wants as long as it means I get to be inside her.

"Fuck me, and give me the courage to walk back inside this building. Fuck me against this building in the alleyway."

My brain doesn't register her words. It doesn't register that this is her saying good-bye. All that it hears is, *fuck me.*

"My pleasure, princess."

I spin her around so she can hold on to the building to keep her balance. I kiss her neck and listen to her groan as I reach my hand into her pants, feeling her wet pussy welcoming me in.

"Fuck me, Killian," she moans. "I can't wait."

I move to unbutton my pants and watch as she does the same to hers. Our need to have each other outweighs our need for safety. I hold my cock in my hand and press it against her bare ass now that her pants are hanging around her ankles. I glance to the right, trying to figure out what people might see if they walk by right now, but since I can barely even see the street in the darkness, I know noone can see us either—at least not until the electricity comes back on, and the darkness disappears.

"Fuck me," she whimpers again.

I press my cock against her again. I grab ahold of her ass and bend her further until I find the entrance to her pussy. My cock slides inside.

"You're so tight, princess," I moan as she tightens around me.

I begin thrusting slowly, enjoying being inside her, but her hips tell me it's not enough. She needs more. She needs passion.

"I need..."

But I already know what she needs. I grab her ass and begin thrusting into her harder and harder. My balls hit her clit with each thrust, and I grab her breast with my free hand.

I feel her building with each thrust. I feel her lose herself, which is exactly what I wanted.

I move my head to her ear. "Come for me, princess," I whisper into her ear before biting down on her earlobe.

"Killian!" she screams into the darkness.

That's all it takes for me to explode inside her.

I tightly squeeze her, refusing to pull out of her anytime soon.

This is what I need. This is what we both need for the rest of our lives. Without this, there is no reason to keep living. Without her, I have nothing. No job. No home. No love. No life.

She takes a step sideways though, and I am no longer inside her. I watch her pull her pants back on, and I do the same. By the time I put my pants back on, she is already turning back toward me. The streetlights flicker back on. She looks beautiful, standing there, in the light. Her lingering orgasm is still shining on her face. Now, we are exposed though, and it is no longer safe.

We both have to make a choice—to go back inside and put a stop to everything or run away together and never look back.

"Have you changed your mind?" I ask.

"No. Have you?"

"No."

She firmly kisses me. A good-bye kiss. A kiss that I refuse to even think about because it is *not* a good-bye kiss.

"This isn't good-bye. If you choose to go back in there, I'm going, too. I'll be hiding in the shadows. I will keep my promise to your father and to you. I will keep you safe, princess."

"You promise?"

"Always."

23

KINSLEY

I OPEN the door to go back inside. I walk in, and Killian grabs the door, following me. I wish he would leave. I wish he were safe, but I guess it's not fair to ask that of him when I won't go somewhere safe for him.

I walk to the far door of the office and pause at it. I can't look back at Killian and still do what I have to do.

"I know. I love you, too. Go. I'll be watching you," he says.

I open the door and step out into the now lit hallway. I quickly close the door behind me. I look back at the door for just a second, and then I start walking. Away from Killian. Away from the only person left who is worthy of my love. And, this time, it feels more final. It feels like this could really be the last time I see him. The last time I kiss him. The last time both of us are alive.

I walk down the hallway to the stairs and down into the dark basement where Nacio told me to meet him. The room is large, and several of the men are already in the room, beginning to load up the money into bags, while others are carrying the bags out of the building.

I spot Nacio and Granddad directing them.

"What can I do to help?" I ask.

"About time you joined us. Where have you been?" Granddad asks.

"I was trying to help arrange transportation, like Nacio asked, but I couldn't find anyone who had a phone I could borrow."

Granddad motions with his fingers, and Santino and Seth grab ahold of my arms before I realize what is happening.

"What is going on? Let me go."

I struggle against the men's hold, but it is useless. Their arms are too strong, and even if I did break loose, there are half a dozen other men ready to grab me. I glance around and notice the whole room is frozen, watching me.

Nacio notices it, too. "Get back to work."

The men immediately snap to life and begin putting the money from the vault into bags.

Granddad walks over to me. "Nacio told me about your trip."

"It's not my fault Killian escaped with the children. I had nothing to do with it. I thought it was in our best interest to keep him alive."

Granddad smiles a smug grin. "I think you had everything to do with it."

I frown. "I was just as drunk off my ass as the rest of them. I didn't have anything to do with it."

"We will see if you have the same story to tell afterward."

"After what?"

My question is immediately answered though.

Granddad nods at Seth and Santino, who immediately

have me on my face against a hard wall. My jacket is ripped off my body and then I feel the sting of the whip.

I cry out, unable to remain quiet.

It hits my skin again, ripping my skin, and causing blood to drip in long streams down my back.

Again.

Again.

Again.

The pain increases each time and I regret ever touching the whip to Killian. I regret what I did to Karp. And I can't help but think I deserve this.

For the hurt I caused.

For being so naive.

For not ending this sooner.

I begin to hear the crack of the whip, but no longer feel it. My back as gone numb. I've tuned it all out, and my screaming stops along with my breathing slowed.

I'm dying. I must be, it's the only reason the pain must be getting better instead of worse. Just a few more minutes of letting go and I'll be gone.

"Now, would you like to tell me what happened on that yacht, or should we try this all over again?" Granddad asks.

The men turn my body to face him, slamming my back against the wall as I scream from the intensity. The pain didn't stop, they just stopped whipping me.

"I didn't do anything. I was with Nacio the whole night. I'm on your side."

I glance to Nacio, who is standing next to Granddad. With my eyes, I beg him to put a stop to this, but he doesn't move. I glance over at Granddad, who nods, and then I'm being dragged back to the wall.

"Stop!" I try to scream, but my voice is no longer able to scream. "Stop!" I try again, this time much louder.

The terror I feel as the whip pierces my skin again intensifies. I understand now why most would rather die from a bullet wound then this slow torture.

I struggle at first, but it doesn't matter. I feel the same darkness coming back, this time much faster than the first time. A shadow casts over my body, I'm going to die.

24

KILLIAN

I sit at the top of the stairs to the basement, listening, but I have a hard time making out what is going on.

Until I hear Kinsley scream. The second she does, I can't wait any longer.

I run down the stairs as I pull my gun out from the waistband of my pants. I know the gun won't be enough. Not against a dozen men with guns, but hopefully, it will be long enough to keep her alive until the FBI gets here.

That's all I need. More time.

When I reach the bottom of the stairs, what I see terrifies me.

I aim the gun at Lee's head, knowing he is the one giving the orders. "Tell them to stop."

He smiles and motions for Seth and Santino to stop. I watch out of the corner of my eye as they jerk Kinsley from the wall. She trembles in their hold, needing their arms to hold her up as blood pours down her back. Santino smacks her cheek, trying to wake her up more, but her seeing me does that for him. She tries to run forward, but they pull her back.

"So happy you could join us, Killian. It saves us the trouble of hunting you down. Now, we can kill you without the hunt."

"Let her go. You can have me. Let her go, and I will ensure the FBI won't find you."

Granddad shakes his head. "I don't think I'm going to have to let her go. We will be long gone before the FBI arrives."

"They will be here in half an hour. You need to leave now."

"I think you are bluffing. See, we have someone on the inside now, and he says they won't move in for another three hours at least."

My eyes widen because he knows the truth. I was bluffing about the FBI. They are most likely still hours away like they told me earlier.

"Let her go," I say again.

"Drop the gun," Seth says as he points a gun at Kinsley.

I immediately drop the gun.

"Kick it away," Lee says.

I kick it.

I watch as Seth forces Kinsley to walk with him over to where Lee and Nacio are standing.

"Give her the test," Nacio says. "Let her prove she is telling the truth."

Lee looks over at Nacio. "And if she doesn't do it?"

"Then, we'll have our answer," Nacio answers.

I look from Nacio to Lee to a broken Kinsley. I know what they want her to do. They want her to shoot me. I want her to shoot me. If she shoots me, she guarantees her life. They will think she is on their side, and they will keep her alive until the FBI moves in. I just don't know how to remind Kinsley of her promise to me.

Nacio pulls a gun from his waistband and hands it to Kinsley. "Shoot Killian. Avenge your father. Prove you choose us, not him."

Seth continues to aim his gun at Kinsley as she studies Nacio's gun for a second. Her eyes go to mine, and I tell her what I want. I tell her to shoot me. Her eyes tell me she loves me.

And then she lifts the gun and pulls the trigger.

25

KINSLEY

I WATCH Killian fall to the ground, and it is the worst thing I have ever watched. I tried not to aim for any vital organs, but watching him fall like he did has me worried. I know it's what he wanted. I know I promised to shoot him. I just never thought I would have to do it.

I feel like I betrayed my heart by shooting him. I feel empty, like I was the one on the other end of the gun.

Nacio grabs the gun from my hand and then tightly hugs me. I wince as his hands hit the wounds on my back.

"I knew you would choose correctly," Nacio says in my ear before releasing me.

Seth lowers his gun, accepting that I am on their side. I smile. This is now my chance to ask about the other locations. This is my chance to become a true Felton. And then I can do anything to keep Killian alive.

But Granddad's laughing distracts me. Nacio lets me go as I turn to face him.

"Is it funny now to watch a man die?" I ask, cocking my head to one side, as I look at my grandfather.

"No, watching you shoot someone because you thought he killed your father—that's what's funny."

"Killian didn't kill my father?"

"No." He laughs again.

"Then, how did he die?"

"I killed him. I had him poisoned."

"Why?" I ask, my voice shaky, as is my entire body. I don't have the strength to stand strong much longer. The adrenaline is the only thing keeping me up on my feet.

"Because he was soft. He grew tired of the business. He grew a heart. He didn't want to traffic people anymore. He didn't want to smuggle drugs. He didn't want to kill people anymore.

"From the second you were born, I noticed when he began to change. His heart simply wasn't in it anymore. Once we found a man to pass the company on to, I thought that would change, and for a while, having Killian there did give him new hope, new energy. Until he found out Killian was FBI. I think he took it as a sign we weren't supposed to be doing this anymore.

"He wanted out. But you don't get out. Not once you start. He had to go, or he was going to ruin everything. He risked everything for you. I had to kill him."

Tears fall from my eyes. "You killed your own son?"

"Yes."

More tears fall. They fall for my father who didn't deserve what he got. They fall for me for losing a father too soon. And they fall for Killian who is barely breathing on the floor all because he sacrificed himself, just like my father did to save me.

"I hate you! I fucking hate you!"

I begin to move toward him, but he pulls a gun and aims

it at my head. I freeze. If I die, shooting Killian would have been for nothing.

"You are just like him. And, now, I get the pleasure of killing you, too," Granddad says.

I glance to Killian, who is lying on the floor. Blood pools around his body, but I can't tell where the bullet went. He's still breathing, just barely. He won't make it much longer.

"I love you always," I say under my breath as I close my eyes.

The last thing I hear is the bang of a gun being fired before the pain in my lungs overtakes me.

26

KINSLEY

I open my eyes, and all I see is white. White walls. White lights. White sheets.

I'm in a hospital room. I survived.

I test my arms and legs, trying to see what has been damaged, but the only thing that hurts are my lungs.

"Oh my God!" Scarlett squeals next to me before she tackles me with her body. "I was afraid you would never wake up. I flew to Paris as soon as I heard."

I smile, happy to see someone I love. Happy to feel safe. I just wish I saw another face in the room as well.

"Is Killian…"

"He's alive."

I exhale the breath I was holding while waiting for Scarlett to answer.

"Where is he?"

"He's here, at the hospital. They won't let him see you until they have questioned you first. And they couldn't question you until you were awake. He's been going crazy out there."

I smile. He's alive.

"Where was he shot?"

"The shoulder. Evidently, your grandfather didn't have very good aim."

I raise my eyebrows, realizing Killian must have said Granddad shot him instead of me. I'll have to remember that when I'm questioned.

"Did Granddad..."

"He's dead."

"How?"

"Nacio shot him. Nacio is in the hospital room next door. The FBI shot Nacio after they heard him fire at your grandfather. He's a rather good-looking..."

"He's a horrible person, Scarlett. I watched him shoot a woman."

"Nacio also saved your life."

"It still doesn't make up for what he did. He will still spend the rest of his life in jail."

Scarlett nods.

"Did they get everyone else who was there?"

Scarlett shakes her head. "No, I guess Nacio's brother escaped. And they haven't found their father or their other location yet. They are hoping Nacio will tell them in exchange for a deal when he wakes up."

I nod. I hope the FBI finds them, but for now, I'm glad the Feltons are no longer involved.

I'm safe. Killian is safe. That is all that matters.

"My mother?"

"She's in jail."

I nod, not really caring.

I hear a knock on the door, and I sit up, hoping it is Killian, but I see two men in suits standing at the doorway.

"We have a lot of questions for you. Are you up for it?" one of the men asks.

I nod. "I bet you do."

27

KINSLEY

The FBI questioning went well. I told them Killian's lie about who shot him even though I'm not sure it mattered. We did whatever we needed to survive. They aren't going to arrest me or Killian. Although Killian will never be able to work for the FBI again. I'm not sure if it matters anymore though.

The doctor came in afterward and said I was in the clear and could fly home. I was suffering from a slight infection. They will keep me on antibiotics and have me check in later in the week to make sure the wounds on my back are still healing, but they don't expect any further complications. I just need to take it easy and not do anything too strenuous for a while. The scars that will remain on my back will be minimal.

Scarlett bought me some clothes. I asked for sweats and a T-shirt, but instead, she bought me a dress and under-wear. It's a nice, simple black dress. Something I used to wear all the time but not something I want to wear on a long flight home from the hospital. I put it on anyway though because it is the only thing I have to wear. I pull a brush through my hair but don't bother with putting on the makeup Scarlett brought me.

A knock sounds at the door, and I perk my head up. Killian still hasn't come in to see me, so I assume it's him.

"Come in!" I shout.

I look up, and my heart stops as I wait for the door to open. When I see it's just Scarlett, I sigh.

"Ready to go?"

"Yes."

She walks over to me. "You look beautiful." She reaches into the overnight bag she brought me and pulls out the makeup bag.

"I really don't think I need makeup to walk out of the hospital."

"I want you to feel your best," Scarlett says. She applies some blush, lipstick, and mascara to my face, despite my protests.

Another knock sounds, and I perk my head up, but when I see it's just my nurse, my head drops.

She pushes a wheelchair into my room. "Your chariot," my nurse says.

I sigh and climb in. I'm too tired to protest that I can walk.

Scarlett gathers my things and then follows us out of the room. The nurse walks slowly down the hospital hallways while I really want her to hurry. I don't know where Killian is, but I need to find him. I need to see that he is still alive. And I need her to hurry up, so I can do that.

We finally reach the front door to the hospital when Scarlett says, "I can get her from here."

I'm shocked when the nurse nods and lets her push me.

"Thanks. I don't think I could stand for her to keep pushing me at that pace much longer."

Scarlett smiles and keeps pushing me. I expect her to push me toward the parking lot, but she doesn't. Instead, she pushes me around to the side of the hospital.

"Where are we going?"

"You'll see."

My heart flutters at the unknown but not in a good way. I don't know if I will ever be spontaneous again. Not after what I went through. I never want to have my heart racing that fast again.

Scarlett suddenly stops the wheelchair. "Do you think you can walk?"

"Yes. But where to?"

She shakes her head and holds out her hand to me. I take it, and she helps me stand in the small heels she brought me.

"Lean on me if you need to," she says.

I hold on to her arm as I get used to walking again. It's not too bad. It just hurts when I breathe.

We turn the corner of the building when I see him.

Killian is standing in a beautiful garden with candles everywhere. He's dressed in dark jeans and a button-down shirt. One arm is in a sling. The beard that started growing is now gone, and his hair is trimmed a little. I don't care what he looks like though. I'm just happy to see him.

Killian runs over to me. When he reaches me, he throws his free arm around me, and I wrap my arms around his neck after letting go of Scarlett. His lips sizzle against mine. His tongue finds mine, and then my world stops.

For the first time in forever, I don't have to think about anything else. Not family obligations. Not my future. Not my past. Not surviving. Or right or wrong. Or saving him.

For the first time in forever, I can just get lost in a kiss.

I don't know how long the kiss lasts, but when it stops,

Killian reaches down to hold my hand. He leads me into the garden that looks so similar to my favorite place at the casino where he proposed earlier.

He stops when we are in the center of the garden.

"Princess, I know this isn't going to be perfect. We are in a fucking hospital garden. We both have a lot of healing to do, but after the last few weeks we have had, I don't think I can wait for perfect. I don't know if I will ever get perfect, so I have to do this now."

I watch as he kneels in front of me, and tears spring to my eyes.

"You are everything I ever wanted. I knew it from the first time I saw your picture, from the first time I saw you in person. When I promised your father I would protect you forever, I knew you were mine.

"You are a beautiful princess, but I've realized now, after really getting to know you, you are so much more. You are my warrior princess. My survivor. You have more strength in you than I ever thought possible. You even had the strength to risk your life for me. To save those children and women. You even had the strength to shoot me even though you didn't want to. You're everything I ever thought I wanted and more.

"I know I'm not worthy. I made a terrible FBI agent. I couldn't even figure out the trafficking and smuggling ring that was right under my nose. I'm unemployed. I don't have any money. I don't know what my future holds. I don't even have enough money to buy you a proper ring. But I can't wait until I do to ask you to spend forever with me. I can't wait because we aren't promised a tomorrow, and I want to start living tomorrow with you now.

"Kinsley, will you marry me?"

Killian opens a box, and in it is a pink plastic ring with a fake diamond on top. Most likely, he got it from a machine in the lobby.

I smile. "Maybe."

"I'll take that as a yes," he says, grinning widely.

Standing, he puts the cheap ring on my finger. A ring I know he will replace when he gets the chance, but this proposal is perfect, and I wouldn't have it any other way.

"Take it as an always."

EPILOGUE
KILLIAN

Six Months Later

I HEAR the front door to our one-bedroom loft in New York open and close.

Finally, I think.

I close my computer and meet Kinsley at the door. She quickly kisses me on the lips, but I can tell she's distracted.

"What's wrong?" I ask.

"Huh?" she says as she smiles at me.

She places her bag on the counter, and I see the shine of her stupid plastic ring reflecting in the light as she does.

I wanted to replace the ring right away, but after the proposal, we weren't sure what to do with the money she had, and I had practically no money. We weren't sure what to do with the Felton Corporation. With our lives.

It took us a couple of months to realize we didn't want to touch any of the tainted money from the Felton Corporation. We didn't want to run the company. Basically, we wanted a fresh start. So, Kinsley sold the company, and we gave all the money away to charity.

Now, Kinsley works for an organization that helps battered women rebuild their lives. She's good at it, and she really seems to love it.

She didn't take long to figure out what she wanted to do, but it has taken me longer to decide what I want to do. I'm just not sure how I'm going to take the job.

"What's got you so distracted?" I ask, holding on to her waist and kissing her neck.

She moans softly. "Right now, you."

I grin. "Good." I kiss her neck again. "Seriously though, are you okay?"

"Yes. I'm just worried about this woman who came in today. I'm not sure she's ready to start over."

I nod. "Be patient with her. It takes time." I kiss her neck again.

"I know, but I don't want to talk about work anymore."

"Me neither. I want to fuck you."

She groans. "Fucking sounds good."

I move my hand under her T-shirt, feeling her smooth stomach. "I want to try something. Do you trust me?"

"Of course. What do you have in mind?"

I lift her up and carry her to the bed. I gently put her down, firmly kissing her on the lips. I walk over to the nightstand and pull out the items I bought today. I hold them out to her. She closely looks at the rope and whip.

"You want me to whip you again?"

"No. I want to use it on you."

Her eyes widen.

"I think it's only fair since you got to use it on me." I lean down and kiss her earlobe before sucking and pulling on it with my teeth, the way she likes. "I think you will enjoy it, but if I take it too far, I will stop."

I've been dreaming about doing this to her since she

held the whip in her hand in Mexico. And knowing she needs to face her fears so the pain of it won't haunt her forever.

"Yes, I want it."

I smile. I remove her clothes, followed by mine. With her laying on her stomach, I tie her arms to the posts of the bed with rope, but I leave her legs free. I lift her legs onto her knees and then kneel behind her with the whip in my hand.

"Ready?" I ask, rubbing her ass.

"Yes," she breathes.

I let the whip come down on her ass. She whimpers, and I watch as her ass turns a bright shade of pink.

"That was—"

I don't let her finish. I use the whip again on the other cheek. She squeals, and my cock twitches when I see her body react to me. I hit her again and see hot liquid dripping from her pussy down her leg. I whip her again and again until—

"Fuck, Killian," she moans.

Then, I can't take it any longer.

I thrust inside her, and she screams. I thrust quickly, knowing how she likes it. I grab her breasts and hear her moans intensify.

"I'm going to—"

She can't speak, but I feel her clenching around me. It's the fastest she has ever come, showing me how much being whipped and tied up turns her on. I thrust faster until I'm filling her with my cum.

After we come together, we both collapse, exhausted and content just to be together. After a few minutes, I feel her wiggling, trying to get out from under me, and I laugh.

"Hold on," I say. I untie her hands and roll off her so we are lying side by side.

She smiles at me. She looks so beautiful, so content, lying naked in our bed. I don't think I will ever get used to the sight.

"What's wrong?" she asks when she notices I don't wear the same content smile she does.

I take a deep breath before I speak, "I accepted a job today."

"Really?" she asks excitedly, sitting up higher in bed.

"Yeah."

"Well...what is it?"

I take another breath, not sure about how she is going to react. "I accepted an executive job with a hotel chain."

Her smile brightens. "Really? That's awesome. That job always suited you."

"You don't think it's stupid, doing the same work I did for your family?"

"No. You were great at it. I don't care what you do, as long as you are happy."

I grab her neck and firmly kiss her, showing my appreciation. "You amaze me."

I turn back to my nightstand and find the box I bought after accepting the job and knowing how much money I will be making.

"I guess I can give you this then," I say, opening the box.

Her mouth drops. "Killian, it's beautiful!"

I smile and take the plastic ring off her finger. I replace it with the large princess cut ring. I go to throw the plastic ring away, but she snatches it back.

"You are not getting rid of that ring—ever," she says sternly.

I smile. "Whatever you say, princess."

"Does this mean we have enough money to start planning a wedding?"

"It does."

She squeals again. "I need to call Scarlett. We need to get to planning right away if we want a shot at a spring wedding."

She hops off the bed and begins walking away, mumbling to herself, but I don't mind. The view of her naked ass is worth her leaving.

She pauses at the door and looks at me. "Now that we are no longer broke, does this mean, in a couple of months after the wedding, we can start trying for kids?"

I laugh. "Maybe."

She smiles. "I'll take that as a yes."

The End

Thank you so much for reading! The series isn't over just yet, Scarlett has a story to tell that you won't want to miss!

Want to order signed paperbacks? Visit:
store.ellamiles.com

You can get the first book in Scarlett's series, Definitely Yes, for FREE here—>
https://www.ellamiles.com/series/definitely/definitely-yes-free

Keep reading for a sneak peek of Definitely Yes...

DEFINITELY YES PREVIEW

Why are there no hot men in this bar? I sigh. *Why are there no hot men at any bar—ever?*

I take a sip of my gin and tonic as I scour the room, looking for anyone who will do for tonight. This bar used to be the best bar in New York City to pick someone up for a one-night stand. Now, it is just another bar to add to my list of has-beens.

It's a shame really. This bar has everything. It's clean; it has a live band every night, not just on the weekends; and the bartenders here know my drink order without me having to order. It used to be full of life, full of energy, but now, it is nothing more than an overpriced bar with crappy music and no hot men.

As I glance around the large bar, I don't count more than six other people in the bar, only two of which are men. One is too old—my best guess, mid-forties—and the other, I doubt he's eighteen.

"It just ain't what it used to be, is it?" Todd says.

"No, it isn't. I hate to say this, but I'm going to have to find a new bar," I say.

Todd wipes off the counter in front of me. "I hate to say this, but me, too. The tips aren't what they used to be. And if my favorite tipper leaves me—"

"Your only tipper and most attractive customer," I say, smiling.

Todd flashes me his smile that is missing one front tooth. "Only tipper. I won't be able to survive on the measly salary this place pays me. I guess it is off to find greener pastures."

"Yeah, I guess." I frown as I finish off the last of my gin and tonic.

Todd immediately places another glass in front of me, making me smile.

"Thanks, Todd."

"You bet, Scar," he says.

I take the full glass and raise it to my lips, sipping the perfect, cold liquid that I find myself needing more and more after a long day of work. I love what I do, but running Beautifully Bell Enterprises, the fashion and beauty company I own, is exhausting by the end of the day. I need something cold to relax me and a hot man in my bed to reenergize me for the next morning.

As much as I love spending my evening talking with Todd, it's not enough. I need more. I need thrills and excitement to invigorate me. To make me excited to wake up the next morning. I used to have that every night when I was twenty-five and a model. I always knew the hippest bars to find an attractive man. Half of the time, I didn't even have to go to a bar to find a man. The male models I worked with that day would more than do.

Now, at thirty-two, I've found that it is harder to find a good man for one night. I don't model as much anymore. I just don't have time with my fashion empire. And then men my age are beginning to become more and more interested in more than just one night. They want marriage and babies and the whole package. I'm just not ready for that yet.

That leaves me with the twenty-something-year-old men who are practically still babies themselves. Men who are excited about the idea of one night only. Men who don't care that I'm older than them. Men who like being controlled by a more domineering woman.

My phone buzzes against the table, and I turn it over to see who messaged me.

Kinsley: Emergency! Can I meet you tomorrow? Have news!

My heart races when I see the words *Kinsley* and *emergency* in the same line.

My best friend has been through too much in the past. It's been almost ten years now since she found out her family was money launderers, smugglers, and killers. Ten years since my best friend almost died at the hand of her own grandfather. Now, she's living her happily ever after here, in New York City.

But seeing her text message has me worried that something has happened again. It's after midnight, and my best friend is never awake this late on a Thursday.

I type frantically.

Me: Where are you? Do I need to call the police? What's happening?

I stare at my phone, gripping it much too hard, as I wait for the message to get sent and read.

Come on, come on, I think as I frantically bounce my legs up and down, hoping that she will respond quickly. *I should have just called her, but what if she is stuck in the back of a trunk somewhere? Then, if I called her, it would let her kidnappers know that she had a phone? What if her mouth is taped shut with duct tape, and she can't speak? What if—*

Then, I watch as three dots appear on the screen, indicating that she is typing a response. My phone buzzes in my hand as the message comes through.

Kinsley: LOL. Sorry, didn't mean to scare you. There is nothing wrong. I'm completely fine. Just have some happy news that I can't wait to tell you tomorrow! We've been having trouble with finding time for each other lately, so I just wanted to make sure you knew that I really need you to drop everything and just be my best friend tomorrow.

I shake my head at my friend.

Me: Chica, you just about gave me a heart attack, and then you wouldn't have been able to share your news with me. Just name the time and place, and I'll be there tomorrow.

Kinsley: Eileen's Cheesecake. 1:30 p.m.?

I laugh at her message. *Since when does my friend think it is a good idea to skip lunch and just go straight for dessert? Sounds like I am finally rubbing off on her.*

Me: Done.

I smile, excited to take a break tomorrow to go be with my best friend. It has been a while since I have seen her. *Three months? Or is it four?*

Even though we live in the same city, we might as well live on different continents. With my busy schedule, it's too hard to find time to see each other. Especially since Killian, her husband, doesn't like the idea of us going out to pick up guys for me at night. I need to change that.

I pull up my calendar on my phone. *Shit.* I have meetings all afternoon. *Not anymore,* I think, smiling. I hit Delete on every single one that starts after one o'clock and then type in *Afternoon with Bestie,* starting at one thirty p.m. instead.

I open my email and type a quick message to my assistant, Preston, to cancel everything and reschedule for later. I also tell him to make sure I have an hour or two in the afternoon at least once a week to make time for my friends. I've worked hard enough these last ten years. I think I deserve an hour or two break to actually enjoy the money I make and spend time with my friends.

I should also think of planning a vacation soon. Maybe see if Kinsley and Killian would want to tag along. I'm sure I could find plenty of men to enjoy my time with if we went to a beach in the Caribbean or Mexico. So, I tell Preston to find a good time in my schedule to do that, too. I hit Send, knowing that Preston is going to hate me when I come into the office tomorrow, but he can handle it. It's my business, and if I decide I need a break, then I need a break.

I feel better already as I take another sip of my gin and tonic. I might not be going home with a man tonight, but at least I can go home, feeling good from the alcohol and knowing that tomorrow is going to be a good day.

I finish my fourth drink.

"Another?" Todd asks although he knows I usually stop after four, my usual limit for feeling good without over-doing it.

"A shot of tequila and then another gin and tonic."

Todd raises his eyebrows at me, but doesn't question me as he goes about making my drinks. "What's got you in a better mood?"

"My best friend has good news that she is sharing with me tomorrow."

"I thought I was your best friend," Todd says, placing the shot and glass of gin and tonic in front of me.

"Best guy friend." I wink at him. I raise the shot glass. "To my best guy friend."

Todd smiles, and to my surprise, he raises his own shot glass. We clink the glasses together and then both down our shots. The tequila burns in the best possible way as it goes down my throat.

My phone buzzes again, and I expect to see a message from Kinsley. Maybe she wants to meet up tonight after all. I doubt she will be able to keep her good news to herself any longer. But it's not from Kinsley. In fact, I have no idea who it is from. I open the text message.

Unknown: I want you, just for tonight. I want to make you feel things you have never felt before. I've been watching you all night, Beauty. You're exactly what I want.

I stare down at my phone, confused as to what is going on. I glance over at Todd, assuming it is a prank, but he is deep in conversation with the older gentleman who is now sitting at the bar instead of at one of the pub tables.

Hmm...

Me: I think you have the wrong number.

My phone buzzes again almost immediately.

Unknown: I have the right number, Beauty. I want to shred into pieces that little red dress you're wearing that hugs your overwhelming curves. I want to tame that mane of long, wavy brown hair. I want to feel your tan legs wrapped around my waist until you dig your black pumps into my back so hard that I have to punish you for the pain you have caused me.

I bite my lip as I stare at the seductive message I just received. A message that seems like it is meant for me. The woman he is describing fits me to a T. I uneasily shift in my seat at the thought of having a stranger stalking me. Someone has been watching me, but I can't deny that the thought of a sexy man trying to seduce me via a text message turns me on. It does—more than I would ever admit to this stranger.

I pick up my gin and tonic and spin in the barstool until my back is to the bar, trying to act as casual as possible as I scan the room. But I don't see anyone new who could be sending this. I sigh. *And how would a stranger get my number anyway?*

Todd.

I turn back around and wait impatiently for Todd to find his way back down the bar to me.

"Did you give my number to any strange men?"

"Nope. Why would I want to give any other man a chance to snag my girl?" He smiles.

I wonder if Todd really thinks that way or if it's just a joke in the same way we tease each other about our choice of TV shows. Todd isn't bad-looking. The only odd thing about him is his missing tooth that he told me he'd lost when playing ice hockey. To some women, that would even be a turn-on. He's about my age, but he's just not my type. Not dangerous enough. And I see him more as a friend than a lover.

I look back at my phone. *If Todd didn't give this person my number, then who did?*

Me: Who is this? Who gave you my number?

Unknown: It doesn't matter who I am. All that matters is, we both want the same thing. One night of danger, passion, and mystery. One night that will forever be burned in your memory. One night that will ruin you, so every time you fuck another man, you will think about tonight and wish he were me. Wish he could thrill you the same way that I could.

I read his message, and it's like he has been reading my thoughts. It's exactly what I want. It's what I *need*. But I still don't know exactly what he is proposing. I begin typing to ask him that very question, but I receive his message first.

Unknown: Will you meet me in my room on the top floor of the Waldorf, Beauty? I want to fuck you until you're so sore that you can't walk without thinking about me tomorrow.

My eyes widen as I read his text. I'm supposed to go to a hotel room without even knowing who he is. He could be planning on raping me. He could kill me.

Or he could give me the best night of my life.

I begin to type, *No*, but then stop. *Why am I even considering this? This is crazy! I can't go.*

Kinsley would kill me if she found out. I wouldn't have to tell her though. It would just be one night, and then I would never see this man again. Whoever he is.

He picked the Waldorf, one of the nicest hotels in New York City. He has money.

What if he is that old man sitting down the bar from me? I glance over at him. I study his jeans and button-down shirt. There is nothing fancy or designer about his clothes. His watch is a knockoff. And he's drinking cheap whiskey. He couldn't afford a hotel room like that.

I could ask Todd to go with me. Check out this man and let me know if he's okay first. But that would take all the excitement out of it.

I reach into my purse, making sure the pepper spray I bought after Kinsley had gone missing is still there. It would be my only defense.

I do a lot of kickboxing to stay in shape. I've taken some self-defense classes. Being a single woman, living in New York City, I felt I needed some level of protection. But I know my skills would be no match for a man who is prepared to rape or murder. If he has a gun, I'm fucked. If he surprises me, I'm fucked. If there is more than one man, I don't stand a chance. It doesn't matter how many classes or how strong I am for a woman; most men are still stronger than me. I shouldn't even be considering it.

I hear the door open, and warm, humid air fills the room. I turn just in time to see a tall, dark man leaving. A man in a suit with tousled hair on top of his head. He looks like any typical businessman my age who works in New York. But there is one thing not typical about him. He turns to look at me just before the door closes, and for a split second, I see the danger lurking in his eyes as he stares at me like no man ever has. A danger that pulls at my heart.

I glance back down at my phone and hit the Delete button until I erase, *No*. And then I type, *Yes*, and send the text.

Grab Definitely Yes for FREE Here:
https://www.ellamiles.com/series/definitely/definitely-yes-free

Definitely Yes
Definitely No
Definitely Forever

FREE BOOKS

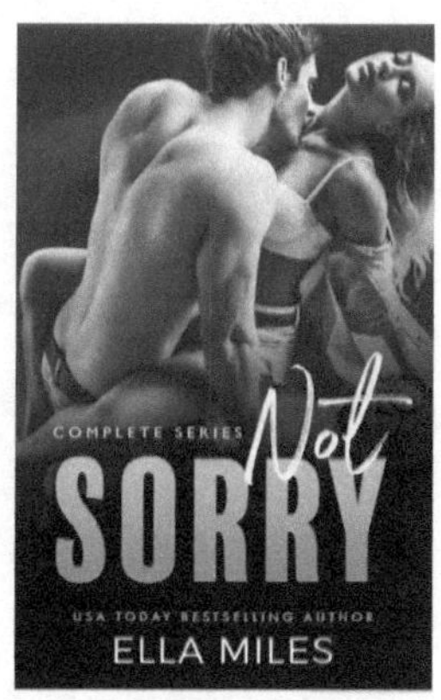

Read **Not Sorry** for **FREE!** And sign up to get my latest releases, updates, and more goodies here→EllaMiles.com/freebooks

Follow me on BookBub to get notified of my new releases and recommendations here→Follow on BookBub Here

Join Ella's Bellas FB group for giveaways and FUN & a FREE copy of Pretend I'm Yours→Join Ella's Bellas Here

Dirty Addiction

Dirty Revenge

ALIGNED SERIES:

Aligned: Volume 1 (Free Series Starter)

Aligned: Volume 2

Aligned: Volume 3

Aligned: Volume 4

Aligned: The Complete Series Boxset

UNFORGIVABLE SERIES:

Heart of a Thief

Heart of a Liar

Heart of a Prick

Unforgivable: The Complete Series Boxset

STANDALONES:

Pretend I'm Yours

Finding Perfect

Savage Love

Too Much

Not Sorry

ABOUT THE AUTHOR

Ella Miles writes steamy romance, including everything from dark suspense romance that will leave you on the edge of your seat to contemporary romance that will leave you laughing out loud or crying. Most importantly, she wants you to feel everything her characters feel as you read.

Ella is currently living her own happily ever after near the Rocky Mountains with her high school sweetheart husband. Her heart is also taken by her goofy five year old black lab who is scared of everything, including her own shadow.

Ella is a USA Today Bestselling Author & Top 50 Bestselling Author.

Stalk Ella at:
www.ellamiles.com
ella@ellamiles.com